No Match

Dave's hand snapped to one side as Clint's bullet sparked against his gun . . .

Even after the shooting had started, Clint hoped to frighten the men away with a minimum of spilled blood. Now that one of those men was dead, the chance for an easy resolution was gone. Clint wasn't about to take time to grieve the loss of a man who'd tried to shoot him, so he climbed into his saddle and looked around for the other two gunmen.

"Leave well enough alone," Clint said in a voice loud enough to be heard by anyone in the vicinity. "You made a mistake in coming after me once. Don't make that mistake again."

With his warning still drifting through the air, Clint left Acklund and Mose behind. Their kind of stupidity was its own punishment.

DON'T MISS THESE
ALL-ACTION WESTERN SERIES
FROM THE BERKLEY PUBLISHING GROUP

THE GUNSMITH by J. R. Roberts
Clint Adams was a legend among lawmen, outlaws, and ladies. They called him . . . the Gunsmith.

LONGARM by Tabor Evans
The popular long-running series about Deputy U.S. Marshal Long—his life, his loves, his fight for justice.

SLOCUM by Jake Logan
Today's longest-running action Western. John Slocum rides a deadly trail of hot blood and cold steel.

BUSHWHACKERS by B. J. Lanagan
An action-packed series by the creators of Longarm! The rousing adventures of the most brutal gang of cutthroats ever assembled—Quantrill's Raiders.

DIAMONDBACK by Guy Brewer
Dex Yancey is Diamondback, a Southern gentleman turned con man when his brother cheats him out of the family fortune. Ladies love him. Gamblers hate him. But nobody pulls one over on Dex . . .

WILDGUN by Jack Hanson
The blazing adventures of mountain man Will Barlow—from the creators of Longarm!

TEXAS TRACKER by Tom Calhoun
J. T. Law: the most relentless—and dangerous—manhunter in all Texas. Where sheriffs and posses fail, he's the best man to bring in the most vicious outlaws—for a price.

THE GUNSMITH

324

BALL AND CHAIN

J. R. ROBERTS

JOVE BOOKS, NEW YORK

THE BERKLEY PUBLISHING GROUP
Published by the Penguin Group
Penguin Group (USA) Inc.
375 Hudson Street, New York, New York 10014, USA
Penguin Group (Canada), 90 Eglinton Avenue East, Suite 700, Toronto, Ontario M4P 2Y3, Canada
(a division of Pearson Penguin Canada Inc.)
Penguin Books Ltd., 80 Strand, London WC2R 0RL, England
Penguin Group Ireland, 25 St. Stephen's Green, Dublin 2, Ireland (a division of Penguin Books Ltd.)
Penguin Group (Australia), 250 Camberwell Road, Camberwell, Victoria 3124, Australia
(a division of Pearson Australia Group Pty. Ltd.)
Penguin Books India Pvt. Ltd., 11 Community Centre, Panchsheel Park, New Delhi—110 017, India
Penguin Group (NZ), 67 Apollo Drive, Rosedale, North Shore 0632, Auckland, New Zealand
(a division of Pearson New Zealand Ltd.)
Penguin Books (South Africa) (Pty.) Ltd., 24 Sturdee Avenue, Rosebank, Johannesburg 2196,
South Africa

Penguin Books Ltd., Registered Offices: 80 Strand, London WC2R 0RL, England

BALL AND CHAIN

A Jove Book / published by arrangement with the author

PRINTING HISTORY
Jove edition / December 2008

Copyright © 2008 by Robert J. Randisi.
Cover illustration by Sergio Giovine.

ISBN: 978-0-515-14553-3

JOVE®
Jove Books are published by The Berkley Publishing Group,
a division of Penguin Group (USA) Inc.,
375 Hudson Street, New York, New York 10014.
JOVE® is a registered trademark of Penguin Group (USA) Inc.
The "J" design is a trademark belonging to Penguin Group (USA) Inc.

PRINTED IN THE UNITED STATES OF AMERICA

10 9 8 7 6 5 4 3 2 1

ONE

It was an easy job. Clint knew that much the moment he'd been asked to do it. Normally, he would have passed on such an easy job simply because it wasn't interesting enough to hold his attention and didn't pay enough to make it worth his while. After all, if someone wanted a parcel delivered, there were services to do such things and plenty of young riders looking to make a few quick dollars.

But when he was asked about the job, Clint couldn't shake his head because there was a piece of sharpened steel being held to his throat.

"I don't know about that, Ned," Clint said carefully. "It's really not the sort of job I do."

Ned Smith let out a sigh and took the razor away from Clint's throat. After cleaning it off on the towel draped over his shoulder, he pushed Clint's chin up and scraped a few more times. "I know you're not a scout or a courier, but there ain't anyone else around to do the job. I asked all the young bucks around town, but they're either more interested in drinking their time away or they'd rather ride south instead of north."

"What about the post office?" Clint asked. "I hear they're real good at delivering things like the parcel you've got. Well . . . pretty good anyway."

"The post office is closed up and my parcel is real fragile.

If it gets broken along the way, I might as well have tossed out the money I used to ship it. Besides, I may not even hear for a few weeks if it does get there or gets lost or whatever. Besides that, there's a balance that needs to be paid upon delivery. That's why I thought I'd hire someone to run it on up into Hinterland for me. You can keep the balance as your fee for the job."

Clint started to sigh again, but felt Ned's razor scraping a few more times along his neck. "Hinterland, you say?"

"Yep."

"Where is that?"

"Right across the border into Oregon," Ned replied as he fell back into the tone of voice he used to strike up a conversation with anyone who sat in his chair and paid for a shave. "Beautiful place, it is! Ever been up that way?"

"Yeah," Clint replied. "I have some business in Oregon."

"Perfect! Wherever you're goin' in Oregon, Hinterland's got to be on the way."

"Is it on the way to Beaver Falls?"

After folding his razor and setting it down, Ned wiped away the remaining lather on Clint's face. "Beaver Falls?"

"It's due west, about ten miles past the California border and within eyeshot of the Pacific."

"Oh," Ned grumbled. "Maybe it's not on the way there, but it can't be too far out of the—"

"I'll pass," Clint interrupted. "How much do I owe you for the shave?"

"You've still got a trim coming up. You did say you wanted the daily special, right?"

Clint looked toward the door to Ned's barbershop as if he were hoping to see a rescue party coming for him. All he saw was a few empty chairs and a crooked rack that held his coat and hat. Sunlight came in through a large front window, throwing a shadow of the lettering Ned had painted upon the glass. That lettering advertised the daily special of a shave and haircut, which Clint had asked for the moment he stepped through the door. Apparently, it was too late to change his mind now.

"I did ask for the special, but—"

"Good!" Ned said as he spun Clint's chair around and reached for his scissors. "I'll give you your trim and you can think over my proposition. You'll stand to make a decent profit for an easy ride."

"What's the parcel?" Clint asked.

Settling onto the stool next to the barber chair, Ned asked, "Does it matter?"

"Of course it—"

"Sit still," Ned scolded. "I've got scissors in my hand."

Settling into his chair as Ned clipped away, Clint said, "Of course it matters. For all I know, that parcel could be more trouble than your fee is worth. It could be illegal."

"It's not illegal."

"Then what is it?"

Ned pulled in a breath and held it as he evened out one side of Clint's hair. Moving his stool so he could get to the top of Clint's head, he mumbled, "It's a piece of art."

That caught Clint by surprise. He blinked a few times and tried to think of something else he might have heard. Deciding his ears were just fine, Clint asked, "You mean, like a painting?"

"Sort of."

Clint did his best to get a look at Ned without moving too much. The large mirror hanging from the wall in front of him made that task a whole lot easier. Watching Ned in that mirror, Clint said, "Well, now you've appealed to my curiosity."

"How about I appeal to your greed? I'll add another ten dollars on top of the balance that's due upon delivery. That'll give you close to a hundred dollars when it's all said and done. Well . . . thereabouts anyway."

"That just makes me more curious. What kind of art are you talking about? And why do you look like you'd rather crawl into a shell than talk about it?"

Glancing up nervously into the mirror, Ned didn't seem any happier with meeting Clint's gaze that way than looking into his eyes directly. "It ain't illegal and it ain't any trouble for you to carry, other than it's fragile."

"You're the one that got me to stay here and listen to you," Clint pointed out. "I was about to leave after the shave, but now you started cutting my hair so you might as well finish. You don't strike me as the sort that would be so rude to not talk to your customer while you're working. I mean, isn't that part of your job?"

"No need to tell me what my job is or isn't."

Despite Ned's cross tone of voice, Clint kept his friendly smile in place and his eyes locked upon the barber's reflection. When he saw the embarrassed way Ned kept glancing at the mirror, Clint had to fight to keep from laughing.

"Come on, Ned," Clint said. "You're squirming worse than a boy at his first visit to a cathouse. What could be so bad?"

Ned looked around at the rest of his shop. Even though Clint was the only customer in the place, Ned glanced over at his window to make sure nobody was about to walk in. No one other than Clint was interested in the daily special, which grated against the barber for a reason other than the lack of business.

"It's flowers," Ned grumbled.

"What?"

Speaking in a sharp growl, Ned said, "The art is flowers. I . . . cut the petals and leaves, arrange them into pictures, and fix them onto a board. Some lady up in Hinterland saw my work when her pa was riding through town and she put in an order. I finished it and she offered to pay triple what I was expecting to get and now I need to deliver it."

Clint furrowed his brow as he tried to imagine what sort of picture the barber was describing. "That sounds . . . pretty."

"Go on and laugh, but it ain't easy to make."

"I'm sure it isn't. Why don't you deliver it yourself? I'm sure this lady and her pa would like to meet the artist."

Snapping at Clint's hair with the scissors, Ned replied, "I got a business to run and I don't have time to—"

"Ow!" Clint yelped as the scissors snipped off a little chunk of his earlobe.

"Dammit. Sorry about that." Reaching for a towel and dipping it in some water, Ned swiped at the little patch of blood.

"It ain't too bad. If you want to go, you can leave. No charge for the trim."

Clint touched his finger to his ear and only found a bloody nick. "Finish the haircut, but slow down some, all right?"

"Yeah."

"So you'd rather be known as a barber than an artist?"

"Folks around here consider painting as something that's just done to walls and fences. If word gets out that I do . . . well . . . what I do with flowers, I'll never hear the end of it."

"Another ten dollars on top of the original offer, huh?"

"And I'll pay for your expense, including one night in a hotel once you get to Hinterland," Ned quickly added.

Clint had meant to accept the job without trying to squeeze the barber for any more of his money. But since Ned offered it up so easily, Clint was certain that Ned's artwork was more than valuable enough to make up for the difference. In the end, Ned seemed like a nice enough fellow and Clint was basically headed in that direction anyway. A bit of extra money in his pockets couldn't hurt.

TWO

There wasn't much to iron out about the details of Ned's delivery. It was a straightforward job that involved riding from one place to another. Ned rattled off plenty of details about his artwork, but most of that seemed to come out in a rush once he realized Clint was one of the few people he could talk to about the flower pieces. All Clint needed to concern himself with was that the art was delicate and not to be dropped. It was also going to be delivered to the stable where he'd rented a stall for Eclipse.

The back of Clint's head was still itching from his haircut when he finished his early supper. Running his hand along the fresh cut on his ear, Clint hoped Ned was a better artist than he was a barber. Otherwise, the man might be out of business real soon.

With only one saloon in town, there wasn't much to keep Clint occupied. He'd only been there for three days and the locals already knew to steer clear of him when he sat at a poker table. The beer served at that saloon tasted more like the barrel it was stored in, which didn't leave many other reasons for him to dawdle. Clint was thankful when he got to the stable and found something waiting there for him.

"This was delivered here," a little blonde wearing jeans and a checkered shirt said as she walked toward Clint. Her boots were just as worn through as any cowboy's, but the curves beneath her shirt made her stand apart from a typical stable worker. Dot had always shown a smile to Clint since he'd first arrived. She'd also kept her short blond hair tied into pigtails, even when she'd stayed with Clint after the stables had been locked up for the night.

The package in Dot's hands was the size of a framed painting and wrapped in brown paper as well as several lengths of twine. "That's from Ned?"

"Sure is. What is it?"

Although Ned hadn't spelled it out as such, Clint knew well enough that the barber wasn't anxious for anyone to know that he put together frilly designs made out of flower scraps. Keeping his poker face intact, Clint shrugged and said, "Just a picture of his shop he wants delivered to Oregon."

"A picture of his shop? Who does he know in Oregon?"

"I don't know. Maybe he's comparing notes with some other barber."

It wasn't a perfect explanation, but it was enough for Dot. She shrugged her shoulders and handed the package over to him. "Well, here you go. Are you fixing to leave soon?"

Clint accepted the package that was all but tossed his way. Doing his best to put it under his arm without looking like he was cradling a baby, he nodded. "I've got business of my own in Oregon. There are some old friends of mine who need someone to watch their backs for a while."

Dot sidled up to him and ran her hands down along Clint's chest. "Sounds exciting."

"Not as such. They're trappers looking to strike out into uncharted territory. I'm a little more familiar with the area, so I offered to go along as a guide."

"More than just a guide, I'd wager," she said as she reached down to touch the modified Colt holstered at Clint's side.

"Things could get rough," he told her. "That's why they want me to go along instead of just anyone with a sense of direction."

Dot's face was smooth and her rounded cheeks made her

look at least five years younger than she was. Now that she was close enough, Clint could even smell the fresh scent of her hair. "Still sounds exciting to me. But I'd prefer it if you stayed around for a while to watch my back."

Clint felt his body responding to her. He hadn't been in town for long, but Dot had caught his eye the moment he brought Eclipse to the stable. Every night since then, they'd been spending plenty of time together. They usually spent some time in the mornings as well. He set the package down so he could place his hands upon Dot's hips. Clint had felt her body plenty of times over the last few days and nights, but the way she wriggled between his hands still put a smile on his face. His smile grew a bit more when he moved his hands down to cup her firm buttocks and pull her closer.

"Does your back need watching?" Clint asked.

"Of course," Dot replied as she leaned back so she could pull her shirt open to reveal a thin cotton camisole. "But you could also watch my front if you like."

THREE

Clint watched Dot's back after all.

He watched her back arch as he grabbed hold of her hips and entered her from behind. She was on all fours in the corner of one of the empty stalls at the back of the stable. Dot stretched out both arms and rested her chest against the floor as Clint slid in and out of her. When she straightened her arms again, Dot snapped her head back and got her pigtails to wiggle against her naked shoulders.

"That's the way," she said. When she felt Clint grab her pigtails and pull her head back a little, she grinned and added, "You know just how I like it."

Dot's pigtails were long enough for Clint to hold like a set of reins. He pulled them back just enough to lift her chin, but not so hard that it hurt her. It was something that took a bit of practice, but he must have gotten it right because Dot had worn her hair in the pigtails every night since the first one they'd spent together. She even had a special little groan that came up from the back of her throat whenever Clint tugged those pigtails from behind. He pulled them now as he drove his cock all the way into her until he heard that moan once more.

Dot nudged her head forward until Clint let go of her hair. As soon as she was free to move, she crawled toward the wall and then turned around to look at him. "So you're really leaving?" she asked.

Clint had to suck in a breath to answer her, but he nodded and replied, "Yeah. More than likely at first light tomorrow."

"Then I want to get a good look at you before you go." With that, she guided Clint toward a pile of loose hay and shoved him toward it.

He let himself fall into the hay and then nestled his back against the rough padding. He didn't have to wait long before Dot climbed on top of him and straddled his waist. Dot positioned herself so Clint's rigid penis rubbed between her legs, but didn't quite go in. She wiggled her hips back and forth as if to tease him for a while before allowing him to fully indulge in what she was offering.

Dot's body was lean and getting close to being considered skinny. Her trim figure was tight and a bit muscular from spending her days doing the work needed to keep her stable running. She had slender hips that were just wide enough for Clint to hold onto them. Her thin arms and legs wrapped around him nicely without feeling too bony. Even her small breasts were more than perky enough to match the rest of her. Little pink nipples stood erect like bits of candy.

"You sure you don't want to stay awhile longer?" she whispered.

"I meant to leave sooner," Clint told her. "I just couldn't tear myself away.

"On second thought," he added as he strained to look toward the double doors leading out of the stable, "we might want to take this back to a bed before someone finds us."

"Worried about my customers?" Dot asked as she reached down to guide him to the wet lips of her pussy. "If someone comes by to peep, we might as well make sure they get an eyeful." With that, Dot lowered herself down until she took every inch of Clint's stiff column of flesh inside of her.

Clint stretched out and placed his hands upon Dot's waist. He rested his hands there without moving her, just so he could feel the motion of her body as she rode him. Dot's strong legs pressed tightly against his hips and her stomach clenched as she ground back and forth on top of him. She kept her eyes on him as her eyes took on more and more intensity.

Clint didn't have to do anything to point. Dot in one direction or another. She slowly built up speed as her hands rubbed up and down along the front of Clint's body. Soon, her hips were pumping in quick thrusts that got faster and faster as she built toward a climax. When the moment was right, Clint tightened his grip on her so he could pump up into her.

The move caught Dot by surprise. Her eyes snapped open and her next breath caught in the back of her throat. She tried to make a sound, but could only gasp as Clint pulled out and quickly impaled her with every last inch of his hardness. Once inside, Clint pulled her down and pushed up into her a little more. Dot's body reacted instantly as her pussy tightened around him and an orgasm swept all the way down to the tips of her toes.

"Oh, God, Clint," she sighed. "Oh, God."

Just when Clint thought her orgasm had run its course, he began to move in and out of her again. Within seconds, Dot's body started to shake again and she breathed as if she'd just run two miles in an uphill race. This time, Dot clenched her eyes shut and leaned down so her breasts were pressed against Clint's chest. He could feel her shaking, so he wrapped his arms around her and rolled over so they were both lying on their sides.

Keeping one arm wrapped around Dot's shoulders, Clint reached down to cup Dot's tight little backside. She draped one leg over his side and buried the other leg into the hay, which allowed her to keep moving without forcing him to come out of her. Both of them fell a bit deeper into the hay, but neither of them noticed. Clint was too busy driving his cock into her again and again, while Dot tried to catch her breath as another climax rushed through her body.

Clint was always amazed at the tightness of Dot's body. From the muscles under her skin to the warm pussy that enveloped him, Dot had a way of wrapping around Clint's body like a second skin. As she let out a loud groan, Dot wriggled just the right way to push Clint over the edge. He exploded inside of her with one more thrust. After that, he barely had the strength to move.

Dot pulled in a deep breath and let it out as she rolled onto her back. "You sure I can't get you to stay for a while longer?" she asked.

Clint let out a breath as well and replied, "I can't even recall why I wanted to leave in the first place."

FOUR

Fortunately, Clint didn't see a good reason why he should hurry away from town as if he were carrying some sort of vital information to a battlefield somewhere. All he needed to do was take a look at the tightly wrapped package that had been sent over to the stable to recall just how important his mission was.

In most respects, Clint was glad he'd accepted Ned's job offer. It was good money and was a whole lot better than some of the other jobs he'd taken over the years. Clint made his preparations, had a hearty supper, and spent his last night with Dot in a real bed. When the sun rose the next morning, Eclipse was saddled and ready to go.

"You sure that's just a picture of Ned's shop?" Dot asked as she tightened one of the buckles of the Darley Arabian's saddle.

Since he trusted her with the saddle and didn't want to mess up such an easy job, Clint tied Ned's parcel onto Eclipse's back himself. After wrapping the parcel in his bedroll, Clint used a few lengths of rope to keep the parcel in place so it could hang over Eclipse's left flank like an oversized saddlebag. He may have gone a little overboard with the arrangement, but that parcel sure wasn't going to fall anytime soon.

"It's just a picture," Clint assured her.

"I don't recall any photographer setting up outside of Ned's barbershop."

Clint didn't have to act to put the annoyed tone in his voice when he said, "I wasn't here when it was taken. All I know is Ned had it done and went on about the expensive frame and glass he got to protect it."

"Fine, fine. That man always was a little squirrelly."

Clint chuckled when he heard that and fought like hell to say anything that might strengthen that opinion of hers. If Ned hadn't seemed like a good enough sort who was paying him so well, Clint might have let something slip about the barber's peculiar flower picture business.

Switching to a different tactic, Dot pulled at her shirt until the top few buttons came loose. "How about we take one more trip to the back of the stables?" she asked. "Just a little tumble before you come back?"

"I need to be going, Dot."

She frowned, but still reached out to slip her hand between Clint's legs. "You sure about that? I know you like to pull my hair."

"You like it when I pull your hair."

"Same difference," she said with a shrug. "From what I can feel, you like it just fine."

It took every bit of conviction Clint could muster, but he took hold of Dot's hand and moved it away from his groin. Quite simply, it was either that or put off leaving town for a good, long while. "I do like it," he told her. "That's the problem. Right now I need to get going."

Dot grinned like the proverbial cat that had swallowed the canary. "I suppose I can allow that. You do still owe me for the stable fees, though."

"After all I've done for you?" Clint asked in an offended tone. "You should be paying me."

For once, Dot was the one caught off her guard. She recoiled and glared at Clint as though she couldn't believe what she'd just heard. "Clint Adams, that was the most . . ."

As soon as she saw the smirk on Clint's face, Dot allowed her words to trail off.

He dug into his pocket with one hand and came up with a bit of cash he'd set aside for this occasion. "Here you go," he said. "It's all there, including the cost of that feed we kicked over."

"What feed? Oh! I remember. You did get a little rowdy there."

Clint checked the knots holding Ned's parcel in place and then gave Eclipse another once-over before climbing into the saddle.

"So . . . you will be coming back?" Dot asked hesitantly.

"Yeah. I'm sure Ned will want to hear his picture was delivered. Also, there might be something I need to bring back for him."

"How long are you going to make me wait?"

"Shouldn't be more than a week. I don't plan on racing into Oregon, but I won't be dawdling either."

Dot smiled and rubbed Clint's leg. "Don't take too long," she said. "Or I might just lose interest by the time you decide to come back."

Clint tipped his hat to her, pointed Eclipse's nose toward the stable doors, and flicked the reins. Dot ran ahead to push the doors open a bit wider for him and then waved as he left. Just as he was beginning to entertain the thought of taking her up on her offer for one more quick roll in the hay, Clint felt the wind rushing against his face.

It was a beautiful morning. The sky was filled with clouds, but they were the thick white kind that didn't do much to keep out the sunlight. On the contrary, those clouds seemed to fill up with daylight and let it trickle down onto the world like water from a fat sponge. The air was warm, but the breeze was cool. It only became cooler as Eclipse broke into a run to put the town behind him.

The big Darley Arabian stallion's hooves pounded against the earth and kicked up dirt with every powerful stride. Soon, the horse's muscles were working like a steam engine to carry Clint northward. More than happy to get such a good start on the day's ride, Clint leaned forward and gripped the reins as his lips curled into a smile.

Oregon wasn't more than a day's ride away, but the trail would cut into the trees soon enough. Better to let Eclipse run at a full gallop while the trail was wide and open country spread out in front of them. Once they got into the wooded areas, the Darley Arabian would be able to move at a casual gait at best. Despite the slower pace, Clint was looking forward to the change in scenery. Already, he could see the tall trees stretching up in the distance and he was looking forward to picking out a quiet stream somewhere to spend the night under the stars.

The directions he'd gotten from Ned weren't extensive, but Clint knew his way around Oregon well enough to find Hinterland. And if he had to wander a bit before making his way to the town, well . . . Clint figured that wouldn't be so bad.

FIVE

Clint had been riding for only a few hours and the trees still loomed in front of him. Every step of the way, he'd felt as if Eclipse was about to charge into the woods before he would have a chance to pull back on the reins. But no matter how furiously the Darley Arabian ran, those stubborn trees only crept forward at a snail's pace.

Mountains had a way of doing the very same thing. They could remain just outside a man's reach for days at a stretch until the man came up to them. Clint wasn't worried about the trick that had been played upon his eyes. He knew well enough that Oregon was still right where it was the last time he'd been there, and he'd reach the trees soon enough. In the meantime, he pulled back on the reins so Eclipse could rest for a bit.

Even after the stallion had slowed to a walk, Clint's ears were still filled with the roar of rushing wind and the echo of hooves against the earth. He settled into his saddle and let the echo fade away. Once they did, he was able to discern another set of sounds.

At first, he thought the sounds weren't new at all. They were awfully close to what he'd heard before, although a bit more frantic. They sounded like horses galloping at full speed, so Clint turned in his saddle to get a look for himself.

Sure enough, there were horses behind him. Three of them, to be exact. The group was tearing along the trail that Clint had put behind him not too long ago. As near as he could figure, Clint guessed those other riders would close in on him within the hour. That time would be cut down plenty if Clint decided to draw Eclipse to a stop and wait for them, but he didn't see any good reason to do that.

Odds were those riders were just on their way to their own spot and using the same trail to get there. Clint wasn't expecting any company, so if his first guess was wrong, there wasn't any cause for him to meet up with them.

Clint dug in his saddlebag and found his spyglass. He looked through the eyepiece and adjusted his angle until he got a better look at the approaching riders. They didn't look familiar, but that wasn't much of a surprise. It would have been a real shock if he did recognize the men thundering in his wake.

"All right, then," Clint muttered as he dropped the spyglass back into his saddlebag and twisted around to face front. "I suppose there's one real good way to see if you boys are following me or not."

Because Eclipse had been with Clint for so long, the stallion responded to the slight tapping of Clint's knee against his side. The Darley Arabian shifted gait to veer a bit to the right, but didn't change stride. That way, when Clint finally did snap the reins, Eclipse took off in his new direction like a bullet that had ricocheted off a rock.

In a matter of seconds, Clint had left the trail and was racing through a stretch of taller grass and fallen logs. Although he urged Eclipse to run a bit faster, he kept his eyes on the ground ahead of him so he could try to steer away from anything that might cause Eclipse to stumble. Every so often, the Darley Arabian would jump or swerve on his own to avoid an obstacle that Clint had missed.

After getting to a clearer stretch of land, Clint turned around to glance behind him. The other riders were still back there, but he couldn't tell whether or not they were responding to Clint's sudden change in course. He rode for a while longer and then turned around again. He didn't even need his spy-glass to tell that the riders had not only changed their course but had also whipped their horses to go faster as well. All three of the men were cutting through a pond that Clint had passed earlier and were closing the distance fast.

For the next few minutes, Clint was nervous. He wasn't actually worried about the prospect of someone following him. He wasn't even concerned that those three men might be out to put him down. But he didn't want one of them to fire off a lucky shot before Eclipse could carry him to the cover of the nearby trees.

Clint stayed low in his saddle and let Eclipse run a good deal below a full run. That way, he could watch for how those three riders came at him and possibly even get a closer look at one of them. If any shooting started, he was more than ready to finish the job.

It wasn't long before the three men matched Clint's wind-ing path and let him know for certain that they were follow-ing him. Before too long, he even heard a few anxious hoots from the three men chasing him. When he heard those ex-cited voices, Clint grinned and patted Eclipse's neck.

"You ready for another run, boy?" he asked.

While the Darley Arabian might not have understood the words, he responded well enough to the slightest touch of Clint's heels against his sides. The stallion got its legs mov-ing even faster until the rumble of its hooves sounded more like rolling thunder.

It didn't take long for the hoots and hollering behind Clint to fade away. Not only were the sounds swallowed up by the pounding of hooves against the earth, but the three riders no longer had anything to hoot about. Whenever Clint snuck a few glances over his shoulder, he saw the other men had their hands full just by keeping up with him.

Well . . . they tried to keep up with him.

Less than a minute after Eclipse really hit his stride, the shots started coming from the three riders. Clint could hear the distinctive crack of a rifle along with a pistol to add to the mix. Only one of the rifle shots came close enough for Clint to hear the hiss of flying lead, and he was too far outside of pistol range for him to worry about that weapon. The only thing Clint had to concern himself with was the outside chance of a rifle shot being fired dead-on from the back of a racing horse. Once Clint circled around a patch of trees and veered around to put the tree trunks between him and the riders, even that long shot was no longer a concern.

Clint let out a sharp yelp and snapped his reins again to push Eclipse even faster. The Darley Arabian strained every muscle he had, but only had to do so for less than a mile. After that, the other three riders were nowhere in sight.

SIX

The trail wound through trees that grew closer and closer together as the path cut deeper into Oregon. The little camp
was set up two days' ride from Ned Smith's barbershop,
which put it within spitting distance of Hinterland. Considering how fast the three men had been riding for the last day
or so, it was a wonder that they hadn't passed Hinterland a
while ago.

The youngest of the three men appeared to be somewhere
in his late teens. He had light brown hair that looked like a
tangled, wind-blown mess even when he was standing still.
A scraggly mustache partially covered his upper lip and his
eyes were narrowed into a constant squint. "You sure this is
the place?" he asked.

Walking in front of the other two men and leading his
horse by the reins, the second man was obviously older than
the first by at least ten to fifteen years. He was tall and as
thick as some of the nearby trees and had a full mop of lighter
brown, almost blond hair. Without looking back, he nodded
and said, "This where the tracks lead, Dave. Stop fretting
about it."

"Well, are you sure you followed 'em right?"

The third man in the group seemed to fall in between the
other two as far as age was concerned. He had a rough face

covered by dirt and dark stubble. His hair was darker than the other's but hung down just past his shoulders. Although the cut of his jaw was a bit sharper, there was a definite resemblance among all three men. Judging by the way the dark-haired man spoke to the younger one, he definitely outranked him in the group's pecking order. "You have such a problem with Mose's tracking, then why don't you do it?" he snapped.

"I don't got a problem. It's just that we ain't seen hide nor hair of this son of a bitch for a whole day!"

"This is the trail, all right," Mose said as he squatted down to get a closer look at the ground in front of him. The big man with the blond hair ran his fingers over the top of the dirt, but didn't quite touch it. "There's the tracks put down by that horse."

"And you're sure?" Dave asked.

"It was a Darley Arabian, for Christ's sake," Mose snarled. "It ain't like you see too many of them anyways."

"And you can tell the breed just by them tracks?"

The dark-haired rider gritted his teeth and locked his eyes with the youngest man. "Unless you got something helpful to say, just shut the fuck up, Dave!"

"Jesus, Acklund," Dave grumbled. "No need to get so cross."

"You're testing me, boy."

"He was born to test us," Mose said. "That's what Ma always said. As far as these tracks go, they're the same ones that we picked up after that Darley Arabian left us in the dust. It ain't as though any steps were taken to cover them."

"That's right," Clint said as he stepped out from where he'd been hiding. "I haven't covered them. If I did, I would have surely lost the three of you a long time ago."

All three of the other men whipped around to get a look at Clint. By the time they spotted him among the rocks and trees he'd been using as a hiding spot, it was already too late. Clint had his pistol in hand and aimed in their direction.

"I'll be damned," Dave said through a crooked grin. "Mose did get it right."

"State your business or be on your way," Clint said. "Whichever you choose, you won't be following me beyond this spot."

Acklund kept his hand on his holstered pistol, but didn't seem rattled enough to skin it just yet. On the contrary, his eyes were clear and focused upon Clint as he said, "We don't intend on killing you, mister."

"I suppose you just came by to say howdy?" Clint scoffed. "Well, howdy. You can go now."

Dave's crooked smile grew a little larger and a little more crooked. When he looked back and forth between the other two men, he didn't find anything that was much to his liking. Acklund shook his head at him, but Dave chose to ignore that subtle warning. "Where is it, mister?" Dave asked.

Clint watched the youngest of the three men, but wasn't about to let the other two out of his sight. "Where is what?"

"You know what we're talkin' about!"

"Why don't you tell me?"

"The thing you're carrying for Ned! Where is it?"

Even though Clint heard those words, he couldn't quite believe them. Fortunately, his confusion must have shown on his face.

"We know you're carrying that package for Ned," Acklund declared. "Just hand it over and we'll be on our way."

"Do you even know what it is?" Clint asked.

"We know it's worth a lot of money and that's enough for us."

"How much money?"

Silence fell between all three of the men in front of Clint. Mose looked cautious. Acklund seemed to be measuring Clint, but Dave was losing his patience.

"It was enough to get that barber worked up," Dave growled. "It was enough for him to hide what he was doing and offer good money to hire a man to ride it into Oregon, so that means it's worth enough for him to pay out the ass to keep it safe. You can either hand over that goddamn package or enough money to make it worth our while to let you go. On second thought," he added as he bared a few more of his yellowed teeth, "you can do both and be real damn quick about it."

"Or," Clint said, "I could do neither."

"What's all of this to you anyway?" Acklund asked. "Are you a friend of that barber?"

"Who I am doesn't matter. What matters is that I let you catch up to me so I could give you a chance to think about what you're doing."

"You let us catch up to you, huh?" Dave chuckled. He looked over to Mose, who was still standing over the tracks he'd been following. The biggest of the three shrugged as if he were about to agree with what had just been said.

"I gave you boys every chance in the world to turn back and let me go about my business," Clint continued. "Since you came this far, it's plain to see that you don't intend on being so smart. You found me. Well done. Now go home while you still can."

Dave continued to glance around at all the other men. The more time passed without anyone saying anything else, the more he kept looking around for something. Soon, his head seemed to be attached to a spring and he looked ready to jump out of his own skin. "I'm sick of this talk! You're outgunned, asshole! Hand over the package!"

Shaking his head slightly, Clint replied, "It's not worth all this fuss, boy. If you knew what it was, you wouldn't be so anxious to get it."

"I don't care what it is! Just—"

Before Dave could finish his sentence, Acklund cut him off by saying, "I do. Show us what it is, mister."

Clint nodded and backed toward Eclipse. He even started to smirk as he imagined the looks on the three men's faces when they got a look at Ned's pretty flower picture. He made it to just within arm's reach of the Darley Arabian before a sudden movement caught his eye.

"To hell with that," Dave snapped as he brought his arm up to sight along the top of his gun barrel.

SEVEN

Clint knew what the kid was going to do just by listening to the tone in Dave's voice. Watching Dave bring up his gun was just frosting on the cake. Even though he'd lowered his own gun to try to defuse the situation, Clint was able to correct his mistake in a fraction of a second. He kept the modified Colt down where it was and fired from the hip. Dave was close enough that a blind man would have been hard-pressed to miss.

The Colt barked once and bucked against Clint's palm. Rather than put the kid down with that single bullet, Clint placed his shot in a spot that was meant to keep Dave from doing any damage in return. When the lead punched through the upper portion of Dave's chest, it hit him with enough force to spin him to the side and snap his arm out like a whip.

Dave was still able to pull his trigger, but his shot ripped into the tops of the surrounding trees. His eyes were still fixed upon Clint, but were wide with pain and surprise.

Both of the shots happened within the blink of an eye. After they'd gone off like a pair of firecrackers, Acklund and Mose came to Dave's aid. Unfortunately for Dave, he'd ridden forward just enough to put his own horse in the line of fire of the two other men.

Mose pulled an old .44 from his belt and jumped to one side so he could get a look around Dave's horse.

Acklund was still in his saddle, so he had a better vantage point. He waited before pulling the trigger of his .38 Smith and Wesson until he had a clear line on his target. Since Clint wasn't about to step in the open for him, Acklund fired a shot anyway.

The bullet tore through the clearing that Clint had used for his camp. The angry hiss of the round was quickly followed by the screech of lead bouncing against stone and a short shower of sparks. Clint hopped around the tombstone-sized boulder and dropped down so he could put as much of himself as possible behind the rock.

"Kill that son of a bitch!" Dave hollered.

"You go around that way, Mose," Acklund said.

Even though Clint couldn't see where Acklund was pointing, he knew that the men weren't about to leave him an easy way out. The men intended on flanking him and there was no way Clint was going to sit still long enough for them to do it. He leaned around the rock and was able to pick out Dave right away. The other two were closing in, but Dave's horse was blocking them from him just as well as it had blocked him from them.

"I see it!" Dave yelled. "I see the bastard's horse!"

Acklund poked his head up and glared as if he meant to shoot Dave himself. "Just get back here before it gets any worse!"

"It's gotta be with that horse. Even if it ain't, it's a fine horse. Hell, I bet it's worth more than whatever that barber's tryin' to hide."

Clint wasn't about to give anyone a clear shot at him, so he remained with his back pressed against the rock. He didn't have to wait long before Dave came stomping straight toward him. As soon as he saw someone step around the rock, Clint swung his arm out to pound the top side of his Colt against the man's shin.

Dave let out another pained yelp, but didn't stop moving. In fact, he staggered another few steps forward until his momentum carried him even closer to where Eclipse was tethered.

Now that he was in arm's reach of the younger man, Clint could see the blood soaking through Dave's shirt where he'd been shot. Something else moved directly behind Clint, so he got his feet under him and abandoned the cover of his rock. Before Clint could turn around, he felt a thick hand drop onto his shoulder.

Mose had a strong grip, but wasn't able to sink it in before Clint twisted out of it and followed through with an elbow to the gut. Letting out a surprised grunt, Mose doubled over and sucked in a breath. He quickly straightened up and showed Clint the angry fire in his eyes. Clint swung his Colt around once more to slam it into Mose's face.

In the meeting between iron and bone, there was no question which would come out ahead. Mose's head snapped back and the fire in his eyes dimmed before his back hit the ground.

"I got it!" Dave hollered as he jumped off his mount to go after Eclipse. "Drop this asshole and I'll meet you back home with the horse and the barber's money!"

Clint swore under his breath when he caught a glimpse of where those words had come from. Somehow, Dave had gotten to Eclipse and was yanking the reins free from where they'd been tied. The young man might not have been in the best condition, but his wounds weren't bad enough to keep him from placing a foot in Eclipse's stirrup and hauling himself up to the saddle.

A horse came around the other side of the rock and Acklund fired a quick shot at Clint. The shot hissed within a few feet of Clint and gave him some extra incentive to keep moving forward. The moment Clint saw Eclipse start to rear up and fight off Dave's efforts to mount him, he shifted his attention toward Acklund.

Rather than take the time to aim, Clint raised the Colt as though he was pointing his finger. He squeezed his trigger twice and knew at least one of those shots was a hit. Acklund cursed and wobbled in his saddle as his horse let out a frightened whinny and bolted away from the gunfire.

With Acklund struggling with his horse and Mose just starting to come to his senses, Clint looked back at Dave. Eclipse had managed to pull his own reins free and was up on his hind legs with both front legs churning furiously in the air. Dave had one foot in the stirrups and was trying to swing his other leg over Eclipse's back when the stallion decided to throw him off. Eclipse had the size advantage, so he was able to toss Dave aside without much effort.

Clint rushed toward Eclipse with the intent of calming the stallion down and picking Dave up once he landed. The only problem with that plan was that Dave wasn't about to land anytime soon. Dave's foot had gotten snared within the stirrup and only locked in tighter after he'd lost his grip on the saddle horn and fallen off the side.

Dave's shoulders bumped against the ground and his arms flailed wildly as he dangled from the stirrup. A good portion of his upper body also hit the dirt, but his instinct to pull his head up saved him from breaking his neck. Even with that bit of luck on his side, Dave wasn't in the mood to celebrate.

"Goddamn horse!" Dave snarled as he tried to reach up for the foot that was wedged inside the stirrup. "I'll get you to sit still!" With that, Dave propped himself up as best he could with one arm against the ground. Eclipse's front hooves pounded against the dirt and were on their way up again when Dave swung his other arm around to aim his pistol at the Darley Arabian's head.

Clint reacted out of pure instinct. Although he'd wanted to try to get Dave away from Eclipse, he wasn't about to watch the asshole shoot his horse before he could get the job done. Standing just outside of arm's reach, Clint aimed and fired in the blink of an eye.

Dave's hand snapped to one side as Clint's bullet sparked against his gun. He twisted around either to look at the source of the gunshot or to get away from it. Whichever Dave had intended, his movement only curled his body in just the right way to make certain his right temple hit a partially buried rock when Eclipse dropped him down again. Dave's neck snapped loud enough for Clint to hear it, and then his entire body went limp to hang from the stirrup like a broken toy.

"Shit," Clint snarled as he reached out for Eclipse's reins.

Eclipse calmed down the moment he saw Clint instead of a stranger trying to take hold of him. Once the stallion had come to a stop, Clint kicked at Dave's foot until it fell away from the stirrup.

From the moment Clint heard the men were after Ned's mysterious, valuable parcel, Clint knew the matter would blow over once the riders saw what the parcel actually was. Even after the shooting had started, Clint hoped to frighten the men away with a minimum of spilled blood. Now that one of the men was dead, the chance for an easy resolution was gone. Clint wasn't about to take time to grieve the loss of a man who'd tried to shoot him, so he climbed into his saddle and looked around for the other two gunmen.

Mose was dragging himself to his feet and just taking notice of Dave's crumpled body. Since Acklund was riding back to the camp, Clint fired a few quick shots at him to spook his horse some more. The animal was still skittish and waggled its head nervously as the bullets whipped past its nose. From there, Acklund had his hands full all over again trying to rein his horse in.

"Leave well enough alone," Clint said in a voice loud enough to be heard by anyone in the vicinity. "You made a mistake in coming after me once. Don't make that mistake again."

With his warning still drifting through the air, Clint left Acklund and Mose behind. Their kind of stupidity was its own punishment.

EIGHT

The town of Hinterland was nestled in a bed of trees and partially surrounded by Knee Bend Creek. The creek flowed along the town's northern side and then hooked south to form Hinterland's eastern border. Sticking to the directions he'd been given, Clint found Knee Bend Creek early that morning and followed it all the way into town. It was a beautiful ride that also made it easy to evade anyone else who might get the idea to track him. Eclipse seemed to have forgotten the run-in with the three riders as soon as his hooves splashed in the creek's cool waters.

Knee Bend Creek led Clint straight to a mill that had a tall, narrow wheel turning within the quickly moving waters. An equally tall and narrow young man tended to the wheel and looked up at Clint as if Eclipse had suddenly been spit up by the creek itself.

"Good afternoon to you," Clint said with a tip of his hat. "Is Hank Mason about?"

"Hank?" the young man asked.

"That's right." When he saw only a dumbfounded expression spread across the young man's face, Clint added, "I was told he works at this mill."

The young man blinked and looked up and down the creek as if for traces of any more horsemen coming from that direction. Before Clint could try to break the uncomfortable silence, the young man opened his mouth and bellowed, "Hank!"

Clint fully intended on tipping his hat again and leaving the young man to shout all he wanted. Before he could move along, Clint saw another man step outside through a doorway that barely seemed wide enough to accommodate him.

The second man was old enough to be the younger one's father. He wasn't exactly fat, but the mill was narrow enough to make anyone look that way in comparison. He wore plain brown coveralls over a slight pot belly. As he rushed through the door, he took the floppy hat from his head and used it to swat the younger man in the back of the head.

"No need to shout, boy! I'm right here." The man in the coveralls then shifted his eyes toward Clint and put on a wide smile. "Sorry about that, mister. Pete's simple, but he didn't mean to be rude."

"He wasn't rude," Clint replied. "Just loud."

"Well, he's simple and loud then."

"This fella was askin' for you," Pete said with a grunt.

Adjusting his floppy hat so it sat toward the back of his head, the older man asked, "You wanted to see me?"

"Only if you're Hank Mason," Clint said.

"I am."

"Then I was asking about you. I've brought you something from Ned Smith." Seeing the puzzled expression take root on the older man's face, Clint added, "He's the barber with the—"

Suddenly, Hank's eyes lit up and he clapped his hands loudly enough to make Pete jump. "Oh, right! Ned! That barber who does them prissy little flower things!"

Clint wasn't quick enough to keep the smirk from showing on his face, so he turned his head as he swung down from his saddle. "That's right," he said. "I've got the picture he made for you."

Pete grinned from ear to ear while laughing in a way that shook both of his shoulders. "Huh. You like flower pictures, Hank?"

"It's not for me," the older man quickly pointed out. "It's for my daughter. She saw one of them when we were riding back from making those deliveries last month. You remember, Pete?

"Eh, of course you don't. Anyway, my Ellie saw that picture in that barbershop and she had to have it. The barber wouldn't part with it, so he offered to make one special for her. Demanded a hell of a fee for it, but my Ellie had to have it. I was sitting on a good sum after making my deliveries, so I gave in and plunked half of it down right then and there. Tell you the truth, I figured I was swindled and wouldn't hear about the matter again."

Clint had only been half listening to Hank's speech. Rather than ask for fascinating details about deliveries and spoiled daughters, Clint loosened the knots that held the parcel to Eclipse's saddle. As he pulled at the ropes, Clint recalled Dave's attempts to climb into the saddle as well as Eclipse's attempts to throw Dave off. Despite all of that jostling, the package seemed to be in fairly good condition.

"That's it?" Hank asked.

Clint nodded as he held it out. "It sure is. If you've got the second half of the payment, I can hand it over now."

"I suppose I should take a look at it first. You mind?"

"Be my guest."

Hank grumbled under his breath as he fussed with the layers of paper surrounding the package like a cocoon. He reached his limit when he finally got through one layer of wrapping to find another one beneath it. "Damn it all!" Hank groused as he reached into his pocket for a small knife. The blade made things a lot easier and soon, Hank was holding the precious artwork in both hands.

Stretching his arms so he could take in the piece, Hank looked it up and down. "This is it?"

Clint stepped over to stand beside the older man so he could get a look for himself. There was a carved wooden frame around a pair of thick pieces of glass. In between the glass was a picture of a serene field in light colors. There were bits of flowers ranging from petals and stems attached to the picture in a way to make the whole thing look more like a sculpture. At least, most of the flower pieces were attached. As Hank rotated the frame, smaller bits rattled around between the glass.

"Which end is up?" Hank muttered.

Pete kept chuckling through his gaping mouth.

"Is that stuff supposed to be loose in there?"

Since the picture still looked good despite the stray seeds and things that had been knocked around along the way, Clint nodded and said, "I think it's supposed to be like that. Kind of looks like the ground when you hold it that way."

"Yeah, I suppose it does. We'll see what Ellie thinks about it."

"Do you have the other half of the payment?"

"I don't keep that money here at the mill," Hank replied as he handed the framed panes of glass back to Clint. "Bring this by tonight and I'll see about it then."

"I could just come back tomorrow."

"Nah, you might as well come to my house. Like I says, I need to see what Ellie thinks. If it was up to me, I'd just be rid of that thing altogether."

"But it's real pretty," Pete said. "It reminds me of my grandma."

"Shut up, boy."

It wasn't difficult for Clint to notice that Hank was having second thoughts about his purchase. In fact, the longer Clint looked at the frame and glass, the more nicks and cracks he could find that probably hadn't been there when Ned had so carefully wrapped it. Placing the frame under his arm before Hank could notice the damage, Clint said, "I probably should see to my horse before conducting any more business. Why don't I come back tomorrow and we can make arrangements from there?"

"Suit yourself. It's your money."

Clint's money sure was in question at the moment. Although it wasn't a fortune, Clint wasn't about to ride all that way and trade shots with three idiot gunmen just to let the money fly away at the last second. He tipped his hat to Hank and asked about a good place to rent a room for the night.

NINE

Hinterland was a small town that relied upon Knee Bend Creek for most of its sustenance. As Clint rode down the largest of its four streets, he saw no shortage of stores selling tin pans and other mining supplies. There were fishing companies no larger than a back room and a pair of saloons catering to whoever stopped by to pull something from the nearby water.

There was one hotel, but it struck Clint as the sort of place that would hold more rats than people. Fortunately, Hank was of the same opinion and had steered him toward a boardinghouse on the opposite end of town. By the time he'd gotten there, Clint was looking at a trail that led straight back out to the woods.

The woman who answered the door was short and skinny as a blade of grass. Hair as black as a crow's wing hung down close to her eyes like dirty straw. When she blinked, her eyelashes brushed against the ends of her hair and got those strands wavering back and forth. "You here about a room?" she asked.

"Yes, ma'am," Clint replied. "Are there any for rent?"

"Of course there are. This is a boardinghouse."

"I guessed as much from the sign," Clint said as he

grinned and nodded toward a shingle hanging over the door
that read, BERNADETTE'S ROOM AND BOARD.

The skinny woman looked up at the sign without responding in the slightest to the playful smile on Clint's face.
Turning back to look at him, she blinked once and said,
"You read it right. Rent's three dollars a night, but that in-
cludes two meals. Can you afford that?"

"Yes, ma'am."

"Good. Come inside."

Clint stepped inside and was immediately overwhelmed
by the scent of freshly cut cedar. There was more than enough
crafted furniture in the front room alone to account for that,
but there were also bowls of cedar chips laying scattered
on almost every tabletop as well as an immaculately kept
rolltop desk.

"My last boarder smoked cigars," the woman declared as
she pushed aside one of the bowls of cedar chips. "I'm almost rid of the stench. You don't smoke cigars, do you?"

"No, ma'am."

"Good. It's a filthy habit. How long will you be staying?"

"Only as long as I need to." Seeing the stern scowl on the
woman's face, Clint corrected himself with, "Probably two
days."

"Two days, then. Meals?"

"At least three a day."

"Your rent only comes with two."

Trying to get the woman to grin had become a challenge
and Clint kept trying to get a little something out of her even
though she seemed hell-bent on maintaining her stony fa-
cade. "What about one meal the first day and the full three
the next?"

"I don't work on averages."

"Two, then."

"Which ones?" she asked.

"The best two of the day. Then again, since you don't
believe in average, I suppose they all must be better than
average."

Despite the fact that it was an awkward joke at best, that

was what finally cracked the skinny woman. When one side of her mouth twitched up for a split second, Clint felt as if he'd just won a bet.

"Let me know what you like and I can cook it for you," she said in a bit of a softer tone. "And I hope it's better than average."

"Sounds perfect," Clint said.

"You need anything else?"

"Not unless you can fix a picture frame."

"What sort of frame?"

Of all the remarks he'd been tossing about, that had been the last one Clint had expected to garner a response. Since he'd been carrying the frame with him after untying it from his saddle, all Clint had to do was point to the cumbersome hunk of wood and glass that was under his left arm. "This one."

The skinny woman leaned forward and studied the frame for all of two seconds. Then she nodded and leaned back again. "What's wrong with it?"

"Just some cracks and nicks from being jostled too much."

"I can fix it."

Clint blinked and held the frame out so she could get a full took at it. "There's damage that I thought I could just—"

"Do you know how to carve designs like the ones in that frame?"

"Well . . . I could get close."

"Less than average, though, right?"

Smirking, Clint replied, "Probably, but it'd be good enough."

"Well, if you want it done right, I can do it."

"How much and how long?"

The skinny woman lifted her chin so she could look down her nose at the frame. After a few shrugs and hums, she told him, "Two dollars. It shouldn't take me more than a day."

"A day?"

"If you want it done right, I can't just—"

"No, no," Clint interrupted. "That's a lot quicker than I thought. You could really do that for me? You can really carve that well?"

"Sure. Who do you think made all these tables and chairs?" she asked as she swept a hand around the overly furnished room. "How do you think I got all these damn cedar chips?"

Clint nodded and handed the frame to her. "Fair enough. Just be careful not to harm those flowers. It's delicate."

"I can see that."

"I really appreciate this . . . uh . . . are you Bernadette?"

"Of course I am," she snapped. "Couldn't you read the sign out front?"

TEN

Bernadette was already examining the frame and whittling away some of the chipped edges by the time Clint got up to his room. The boardinghouse had four rooms upstairs and only three of them were for rent. Since there was nobody else renting at the moment, Clint was given the key to room number one.

A quick look into the other rooms made Clint wish he could switch to room number two, but he could already hear the precise little woman downstairs fretting about that one. Rather than try to come up with a good reason as to why he wanted to switch, Clint dumped his saddlebags into room number one and was done with it. There was a bed, a bureau, a washbasin, and no less than three ornate wooden stools in that room. Just being in the immaculate setting made Clint feel like a stretch of dirt road, so he walked back down the stairs to where Bernadette was working.

"Would I be able to get a bath here?" he asked.

"You can get a bath across the street. That is, if you'd rather have me working on this frame instead of boiling water."

Rather than take the chance of accidentally upsetting Bernadette any further, Clint told her to keep working as she pleased while he went across the street. The place she'd recommended was an old building that was twice as long as it was wide. There, several tubs were tended by a young girl who carried buckets back and forth from another room.

The girl was pretty and had full lips, but fell just a little short where age was concerned. She couldn't have been far into her teens, but Clint got the sense that she may have been a little younger than that. She could have been a little older, but he didn't want to take a chance on stepping out of line. The way she lingered to watch him every time she brought another batch of hot water only made Clint's decision that much harder to keep.

Despite all his good intentions, Clint was unable to help himself when she came in the final time. She wasn't even carrying a bucket for this trip.

"Can I get you anything else, mister?" she asked. "Anything at all?"

Clint was glad for the soap suds gathering on top of the water, because parts of him were answering before his mouth had a chance to form a single word. In the end, it was the girl's smile that told him what he'd needed to know. It was a bit too wide and a bit too anxious to be on the face of a woman instead of a girl.

"Actually, I could use some towels," he told her.

"Is that all?" she asked.

"Yeah, it's all," muttered the burly man who ran the bathhouse. Glaring at Clint, he added, "She is only sixteen, after all."

Clint held up his hands. "I only asked for towels."

"Sixteen's old enough, Uncle Jake!" the girl whined. "Sylvia got herself married at sixteen."

"That's Sylvia, not you. Go on and git!" Once the girl had huffed away, the burly man set his sights once more upon Clint. "Someone's been askin' for you."

Clint sat up and immediately looked toward his holster, which hung from the back of a nearby chair. "Who's been asking for me?"

"I don't know. Some fella says he wants to have a word with you."

"Just one?"

"I ain't no messenger!"

"What did you tell them?" Clint asked.

The burly man sighed and turned around to look. Judging by the aggravation on his face, it was hard to tell whether he was looking at Clint or the girl who was still complaining loud enough to be heard from another room. "Hell, it may not even be you they was after. You already paid for the bath, so you can see yerself out."

Before Clint could ask any more questions, the burly man had turned and walked away. Clint hopped out of the tub and reached for his clothes. Just as he got ahold of his shirt, he caught the young girl peeking at him from behind the canvas flap separating his room from the others.

"You . . . wanted some towels?" she asked as she did a poor job of keeping her eyes above Clint's waist.

"Damn it, Sylvia!" Uncle Jake bellowed.

The girl made a face and threw the towels she'd been holding at Clint before stomping away.

Clint dried off, got dressed, and buckled on his holster. Rather than go straight out through the door that led to the street, Clint looked at Uncle Jake and asked, "Is there a side door out of here?"

"Right behind me," he said while hooking a thumb over his shoulder. "Be quick about it."

It seemed that just leaving the bathhouse was enough for the burly man, since no more questions were asked. Clint left by the side door and immediately had to step over a puddle that was almost deep enough to drown a grown man. The building next to the bathhouse was more of a tent supported by a wooden frame, which meant the puddle leaked well under that place as well. For Clint, that meant there were plenty of other feet splashing around in that spilt bathwater to cover the sound of his own as he hurried toward the street.

Clint kept his hand upon the grip of his Colt and his eyes peeled for any familiar faces. Before he could think twice about being so suspicious, Clint spotted just what he'd been concerned about: two men riding down the street leading a third, riderless horse behind them. One of the riders was bigger than the other, but Clint wasn't able to get a close look at either of their faces before they moved along.

Clint leaned out and eventually stepped from between the buildings, then let out a breath. When he felt a hand slap against his shoulder, he spun around and drew his Colt in one swift motion.

ELEVEN

Pete's mouth gaped open more than usual. He shook his head and started to back up in a frantic effort to get away from Clint's gun. As soon as he saw who'd gotten so close, Clint lowered the Colt and dropped it back into its holster.

"Jesus, Pete, you shouldn't sneak up on someone like that."

"I asked if you was in there and Jake said yes," the simple young man replied. "I didn't mean to put a fright into you."

"Don't worry about it. So you were the one asking about me?"

"Uh huh."

After waiting a few seconds in silence, Clint asked, "So what did you want?"

"Oh. Hank wanted to invite you to supper."

"Actually, tomorrow would be better," Clint replied. "Can you tell him that?"

Pete stared at Clint as if he'd just been asked to stand on his head and twirl. "He says supper is at six o'clock."

"What about tomorrow?"

"Six o'clock is tonight."

Realizing the conversation wasn't going to go much further than that, Clint nodded and patted Pete on the shoulder. When the younger man flinched at that simple movement,

Clint felt even worse for drawing his gun on the boy in the first place. "All right. Where do I go at six o'clock?"

His face brightening at the more familiar question, Pete pointed toward the end of town farthest from the creek. "Hank lives in a blue house straight down that way."

"The blue one, huh?"

"That's right."

"Sounds good to me. I'll be there at six."

"I'll go tell Hank," Pete said eagerly. "Oh, do you want ham or cobbler?"

Clint squinted as he tried to make sense of what that question truly meant. His first instinct was to say, "Both sound fine."

"Good, 'cause that's what Ellie's cooking." With that, Pete threw Clint a cheerful wave and took off running down the street.

It had been Clint's intention to put Hinterland behind him as quickly as possible. He had business in Beaver Falls that he was much more eager to conduct than delivering some bunch of pressed flowers. It wasn't even the money that kept him in town. If he hadn't gone through so much trouble already, Clint would have left instructions for Bernadette to deliver the frame when she was done and he could wash his hands of the whole thing.

But Clint had gone through some trouble to get this far. He'd ridden out of his way, had made it all the way to Hinterland, and had even been shot at in the process. In his mind, leaving without tying up such an easy job would have made these last few days one big waste of time. Clint didn't like wasting time. He knew all too well that no man could afford to waste such a valuable commodity.

Now that it seemed he needed another few days to finish this job properly, he figured he should send word to Beaver Falls that he was going to be late. Hinterland wasn't a very big place, but there were some wires leading into one of the buildings at the edge of town. Clint followed the wires past a clean looking stable and to a large shed marked by a sign that read, WIRE SERVICE.

The man who worked the telegraph was large in every respect. He had large arms connected to large shoulders. A large chest puffed out over a large belly. Even his head was large, which worked out well because the smile he wore needed plenty of room.

Holding up the form Clint had filled out, the telegraph operator said, "Clint Adams, huh?"

"That's right. How long before that arrives in Beaver Falls?"

The operator consulted a sheet of paper tacked to a board beside his apparatus and replied, "Beaver Falls don't have a wire of their own, but there's one in the next town over. I go there quite a bit, so I know it shouldn't take more than an extra day. Could be less if someone's already headed in that direction."

"All right. Would you send this for me?" Clint waited for a few seconds, but wondered if he'd forgotten something when the operator didn't say anything back to him. "If I need to pay first, I can do that."

"Oh, it ain't that. Do you know who you are?"

Clint felt a knot form in his stomach at the prospect of someone calling him out for being the Gunsmith. The telegraph operator didn't look like a fighting man, but that didn't mean he hadn't heard some wild rumors or known someone who had crossed Clint's path and not lived to see the next morning. As the muscles in his gun arm tensed for a quick draw, Clint said, "I know who I am. What of it?"

"You're the Gunsmith, ain't you?"

"Yes."

The operator paused for another second, which was just enough time for Clint to see if he was heeled or not. As far as Clint could tell, the only thing the operator brandished was a pencil and paper.

"You remember a fella by the name of Zeke Brockman?" the operator asked.

"Can't say as I do."

"Zeke drives shipments for Wells Fargo. Mostly rides the trail between Omaha and Dodge City. He was damn near killed in a shooting a year or so back when some bunch of wild, gunslinging assholes tried to rob his shipment. You and one sheriff's deputy rode in to clean those assholes out. Saved Zeke's life in the process."

The knot in Clint's stomach loosened. Although he didn't recall Zeke by name, he sure recalled trading shots with those robbers. "There was a whole posse after those men when I signed on. Me and that deputy were all that was left by the time we caught up with those desperadoes."

"Well, that's all that was needed. I gotta take your fee to send this message on account of this ain't my business. But ol' Zeke would string me up if I didn't buy you a drink."

"Oh, no need for that," Clint protested.

"Hogwash! I'm closing up shop right now and I intend on heading down to the Howlin' Moon for a drink. I sure as hell don't intend on drinkin' alone. Not when the one and only Clint Adams is in town. At least let me treat you to some whiskey as a way to say thanks. Zeke may be a pain in the ass, but he's family and you kept him alive."

"The thing is, I'm not partial to whiskey." When he saw the good-natured scowl on the operator's face, Clint added, "But a beer or two might just do the trick."

"A beer or two it is!" the operator said as he slapped Clint on the shoulder. "Let me get this message sent and we'll tip a few mugs!"

If the operator hadn't been so good at his job, Clint might have been able to get out of there before he was done. As it turned out, the big man's fingers flew and the message was quickly tapped out. From there, the operator draped a hand over Clint's shoulder and practically shoved him outside so he could lock up the office.

The operator didn't lose one bit of his enthusiasm on the way to the saloon. When he pushed open the batwing doors, he announced, "This here's my friend, Clint Adams! He's a damn hero and I wanna buy him a drink!"

Clint wasn't about to refuse an offer like that.

TWELVE

The Howling Moon Saloon was a run-down place with a sagging roof. Because of that, there were more posts propping the ceiling up than columns in front of a Greek temple. Between the small round tables, rickety chairs, and thick wooden posts running from floor to ceiling, there was barely enough room to walk. A few of the drunks in the place raised their glasses to the telegraph operator's announcement, but not everyone in the saloon was in such a festive mood.

Acklund was already leaning to his left on account of the deep gouge that Clint's bullet had ripped through his right hip. The wound looked messy, but had mainly passed through meat without doing any serious damage. Wincing as he was forced to lean toward his left to get a look around the post directly in front of him, Acklund scowled and swore under his breath.

"What's the matter?" Mose asked from the other side of Acklund's table.

When he saw Mose start to turn around to look toward the bar, Acklund growled, "Sit still. That son of a bitch that killed Dave just walked in."

That got Mose twisting around even faster. "Where? I wanna—" Even though he easily had fifty pounds on

Acklund, Mose was stopped cold by a quick backhand from the other man.

"Keep still before he sees us."

"Who cares if he sees us? Ain't we here to kill the bastard?"

"Not when he's surrounded by half a dozen of his friends," Acklund said. "We ain't about to make a stupid mistake like the one that got Dave killed."

"Dave may have been stupid, but he was our brother," Mose pointed out "I want to get a look at this asshole's face to make sure we came to the right spot."

"It's him, all right. Didn't you hear that fat man shouting his name?"

"I never caught the name."

"It's Clint Adams," Acklund snarled as though the last two words were vulgarities. "That's the man that the barber hired to carry that package and that's the one that killed Dave. I'm looking at him right now."

Mose gripped the table with both hands. His knuckles whitened as if he intended on breaking the table apart, but he refrained from turning toward the bar again. "When are we gonna go after him? After he sets foot outside this place?"

"We need to be sure before we do a damn thing," Acklund said. "He nearly killed the three of us when he was alone."

"So we just let him get away with killin' Dave?"

As Mose started to raise his voice, Acklund bared his teeth like one wolf putting another member of its pack into its place. Mose quieted down, but didn't look happy about it.

"We didn't come into this saloon looking for a fight," Acklund explained. "My hip's still bleeding and you've had too much to drink."

"I can hold my liquor, goddammit," Mose slurred.

"We want to kill that murderer, not give him a free shot at one or both of us. We can take him out whenever we like. We got the upper hand."

"How do you figure?"

"He doesn't know we're here."

Mose furrowed his brow and shifted toward the bar. He

caught himself before being reprimanded and lowered his head once more. "He's right there. We can take him."

"All he needs is one man to get him to look our way before we get there. Hell, that barkeep's been watching us since we got here and they know we're heeled. If we play this right, we can wait for the perfect spot and pick him off whenever we please."

"We may not get a better chance than this," Mose growled.

"We weren't even expecting to find him yet. We just came here for a drink before picking up his tracks again, remember?"

Reluctantly, Mose nodded.

"Then keep your head down and your mouth shut. If we catch his eye too soon, we'll have to fight him and God knows how many of his friends. We'll get our chance and when we do, we'll see to it that son of a bitch gets what he's got comin' for killing our little brother."

Mose smiled. It wasn't a pretty sight.

THIRTEEN

All things considered, Clint was lucky to have run into the telegraph operator when he did. The big fellow may have been a little loud, but he was friendly and true to his word. He ordered several beers for both of them over the next hour or so and refused to let Clint pay for a single one. Just when Clint was beginning to feel the effect of the beer, the telegraph operator needed to lean on the bar to keep from falling over.

"I think you've had enough, Ben," the barkeep said.

The big man slapped the bar and replied, "The hell I have. Did I mention that this man here—"

"You mentioned it, once or twice by now," Clint said before Ben could go off into another round of his stories. Even though the tales were overblown in Clint's favor, there was only so much he could take. Judging by the grateful looks on the faces around him, Clint wasn't the only one who'd tired of those somewhat exaggerated accounts.

"Yeah, well I jus' wanted to thank you on behalf of my uncle."

"I thought Zeke was your cousin."

"He is," Ben replied. "What did I say he was?"

"Why don't you tell him all about it?" Clint said as he nodded toward the barkeep. "I've got an appointment for dinner."

The barkeep's eyes widened and he started to shake his

head as Ben leaned in his direction. As soon as the big telegraph operator's bloodshot eyes were trained on him, the barkeep put on a well-practiced smile and said, "You mentioned Zeke plenty of times, Ben. I'm sure Clint won't just leave you here."

Clint chuckled at the beleaguered expression etched onto the barkeep's face. "Actually, I was going to do just that. I think the big fellow will be safe enough where he is."

"Sure," the barkeep grumbled.

"All right, then." Digging out some money and handing it over to the barkeep, he added, "This is for the next few cups of coffee along with your patience."

The barkeep took the money and tucked it into his shirt pocket with a smile. "I've seen Ben off before. I can do it again."

"Where the hell you going, Adams?" Ben roared. "I wanna hear all about what happened when you gunned down them robbers."

"I already told you about it. Twice, in fact. I've got to go."

"Where you going?"

"I'm having supper at . . ." Clint had to stop for a second to fight through the bit of haze in his head. The beer was just potent enough to make him pause before remembering the name he was after. "Hank Mason's place. I've got some business with him, and his daughter is supposed to cook supper."

"Ellie Mason, eh?" Ben chuckled. A lewd grin spread across his face as he looked at the other men surrounding him. A few of them merely nodded, but the drunker of the bunch looked just as lecherous as Ben. "I'll want to hear all about it when you come back."

Knowing that Ben was attempting to make a crude joke, Clint slapped him on the shoulder as if the comment had served its purpose. "I will, Ben. Thanks for the drinks."

In the short time he'd been in the saloon, Clint had also managed to swap a few stories with some of the other locals inside the place. He said his good-byes to them and promised to stop by real soon. As he turned toward the door, his

eye was caught by a pair of men sitting behind several posts
at one of the back tables. Before Clint could get a better look
at the men, he was spun back around to face the bar.

"Where you goin'?" Ben grunted. "You need to tell me all
about—"

"I will," Clint interrupted as he bolted for the door. Even
though he made it outside the Howling Moon, Clint could
still hear Ben's voice bellowing from within the saloon. He
quickened his steps before the big man charged outside to
lasso him back to the bar.

Clint took a few steps down the street and stopped. The
sun was on its way down, but the growing shadows weren't
what threw him off his mark. He'd only been in town for a
matter of hours and had barely walked down two streets in
that time. He took a quick look over his shoulder to make sure
he was headed in the right direction to get to Hank's house.

When Clint turned, he spotted a man stepping out of the
Howling Moon. He couldn't make out the man's face,
though, and when the man turned around and went back inside, Clint followed suit by going about his own business.

Foremost in his thoughts was the hope that Hank's daughter was a good cook.

FOURTEEN

The sun dipped below the horizon and several of the windows in Hinterland started to flicker with the warm glow of candles or lanterns behind them. The wind blew in from the west, carrying a cold chill along with them that cut like a blade as they blew to the east. There wasn't much of a moon showing that night, which made it easier for Acklund and Mose to creep up to the large blue house on the edge of town.

Stopping on the edge of the light being thrown onto the ground from one of the side windows, Acklund hunkered down and waved for Mose to do the same. Mose was a lot bigger than his brother, but he crouched down as much as his long legs would allow.

"Stay here and keep watch," Acklund whispered. "If anyone comes toward us, just whistle."

Mose nodded and moved away from the house so he could stand against a tree. In the darkness, he looked like just another bulky shadow.

Acklund kept so low that he was almost crawling when he approached the house. The window he crouched beneath was rectangular and stretched lengthwise along a good portion of the side wall. He removed his hat, pressed his other hand against the wall, and then slowly lifted his head until he could peek through the bottom of the window.

Just then, someone's voice came from the house.

"You sure you don't want anything stronger than that?" it asked.

Acklund's hand flinched toward the gun at his side, but he stopped short before drawing it. Once that initial reflex had passed, he noticed that the window in front of him was partially open and the voice he'd heard wasn't directed at him. Just to be safe, he froze in his spot and listened as intently as he could.

"Water is just fine," another voice replied. Acklund recognized this one as Clint's, since he'd spent a good while listening to Clint back at the Howling Moon.

"Suit yourself," the first voice said in a gruffer tone. "I always like some whiskey to go along with my supper."

There was some further banter, but Acklund was more concerned with the clomping of boots moving away from the window. Once the steps had faded enough, Acklund eased himself upward again so he could take a look inside.

As soon as he was able to see over the windowsill, he caught a whiff of burnt corn bread and boiled beef. The food may not have been perfect, but after so many days of eating beans and jerked venison, it smelled good enough to get his stomach rumbling. He might have been thinking a bit too much about food, since Acklund didn't hear the lighter set of footsteps until the woman making them crossed in front of the window.

When the woman appeared in front of him, Acklund dropped to one knee and pressed himself against the side of the house. Even though he couldn't see the woman directly above him, he was close enough to feel the heat from her body as she pulled the window all the way open and leaned forward a little.

Acklund moved his fingers around his pistol so slowly that he could feel every joint creak within his hand. When the gun brushed against the holster and made the subtle sound of iron brushing against leather, he gritted his teeth and prepared for the worst.

•   •   •

Hank sat in his chair and let out an impatient sigh. "Ellie." He grunted. When he didn't get a reply, he rolled his eyes and turned to look halfway over his shoulder. "Ellie, what in the devil are you doin'? The spuds are probably cold by now!"

"I thought I heard something, Daddy," she replied from the kitchen.

Shaking his head, Hank ripped the napkin from where it had been dangling from his collar and slapped it onto the table. He then got up and stormed to the kitchen as if he were trying to stomp out a fire. "What the hell are you talking about now? If you made me get up for another rodent scraping at the wall, I swear . . ."

"Never mind!" Ellie said. "It's probably nothing."

Hank remained in his spot, half standing and half crouching over his chair. When he didn't hear anything else after that, he lowered himself back down again. Looking over to Clint, he explained, "She gets like this sometimes. Her Ma used to be fidgety, too."

"It's quite all right," Clint said. "Everyone's ears plays tricks on them sometimes."

Ellie emerged from the kitchen holding a large platter in both hands. "Thank you very much, Mr. Adams," she said. "It's nice to know I'm not crazy."

Clint stood up and smiled when Ellie entered the room. She was average height for a woman and had long hair that was pulled back and tied behind her head. For most of the time, her hair looked to be a dark shade of brown. When she turned her head just the right way and the light hit her at just the right angle, there seemed to be shades of red mixed in among the soft, flowing strands. At those times, Ellie looked more like a portrait that had come to life than just a simple miller's daughter.

"Since Mr. Adams is the polite one here," she said, "he can have the first helping."

Hank let out a grunt and muttered, "If this is anything like the last few meals you cooked, he's welcome to it."

Although her expression barely showed it, Ellie was obviously stung by that remark.

"It looks and smells wonderful," Clint said. "I'd be honored." He was laying it on a bit thick, but Ellie didn't seem to mind. She smiled warmly right back at him and set the platter down so it was closer to his spot at the table.

"Thank you, Mr. Adams," she said.

"Do me a favor. Call me Clint."

She didn't seem to mind that, either.

FIFTEEN

The beef had been boiled a bit too long and without quite enough spices, but it filled Clint's stomach well enough. The potatoes had been mashed a bit too much and the cornbread was definitely burnt, but Clint ate his helpings without any trouble. He'd had a lot worse and the company was good enough to make up for the rest. At least, Ellie's company was good.

"So where's this damn painting or whatever it is?" Hank grunted through a mouthful of beef.

"It's not a painting," Ellie said. "It's more of a sculpture. Actually, it's like a little piece of nature all framed and—"

"It's an overpriced bunch of flowers glued to some paper," Hank cut in. "At least it'll be worth something, right?"

Rather than look at her father, Ellie kept her eyes fixed upon Clint. Her slight wince at his words may not have distracted Hank from his supper, but it would have been more than enough to tip any cardplayer off that whatever she said next was going to be a lie. "Sure," she said. "Most works of art are valuable."

Before Hank could say anything to that, Clint added, "And they usually gain value as time goes on."

"Really?" Hank asked as he looked over at Clint with renewed interest.

Clint had put his two cents in as a way to take some of the heat from Ellie. Now that Hank actually seemed interested, Clint felt as if he'd painted himself into an awfully tight corner. "Yes. Once that artist gets known for, uhh, what he does . . . his works become . . . rare."

It wasn't the best choice of words, but they did the trick. It helped that Hank was only halfway listening in the first place, so hearing enough terms thrown his way got him nodding and shifting his focus back onto his plate.

"I suppose," he grunted. "Just don't expect me to buy any more of the damn things."

"I won't, Pa," Ellie said. "This will be just fine."

"How do you know that?" Hank asked as he shifted his critical eye toward Clint. "You ain't even seen it yet. Why didn't you bring it along with you, again?"

"It's like I said when I first got here," Clint explained. "There were a few things to touch up. After all, you wouldn't want me to hand it over before it looks its best would you?"

"No," Hank grumbled. "I suppose not."

"There you go, then. It should be all fixed up in a day or so."

Hank's head snapped up. "Fixed up? Was it broke?"

"No. It's just . . ."

"I know what you mean, Clint," Ellie said. "I don't mind waiting, Pa. That's the way these things are done."

Suddenly, Hank waved at them both as if he'd been surrounded by horseflies. "Fine! Good! I'm just sick of talking about the damn thing. I wanted you to come over so I could get the rest of that money to you, but I don't feel right payin' when I don't have the . . . whatever the hell it is . . . in my hands."

"I understand," Clint said with a solemn nod.

"Good. I expect to have it in another day or so, just like you said. Otherwise, I might be inclined to ask for a discount on the price. After all," Hank said, "this whole damn thing took too long anyways."

"I agree."

That last statement from Clint took some of the wind from

Hank's sails. He looked across the table, trying to get himself as riled up as he'd been moments ago. Unable to do so, Hank let out a disgruntled breath and pushed away from the table. "I'm gonna step outside for a smoke."

Hank's boots smacked against the floor until they carried him through the front door. Once outside, the older man punished the porch in a similar fashion.

After a few seconds, Ellie said, "You can go outside if you want. He's never as cross as he sounds."

"No," Clint replied. "I think I'd rather stay inside."

"I was just going to clean up."

"Sounds like fun."

SIXTEEN

Now that her father was outside, Clint had a good chance to see Ellie. Hank didn't exactly overshadow her and he certainly didn't intimidate Clint. The fact of the matter was that Ellie simply chose to fade into the background when her father was in eyeshot. Now that he was away, she could relax and shine a bit.

In fact, Ellie shined quite a lot. Her features were simple, but not plain. Her skin was smooth and her hair had a feathery quality. Her little nose and high cheekbones made her even more attractive when she smiled and at the moment, she was smiling very wide indeed.

"What's the matter?" Clint asked.

The two of them stood side by side in the kitchen. Ellie washed the dishes in a large basin and Clint dried them. Handing over another of the dishes, she shrugged and said, "You're embarrassing me."

"How?"

"You're . . . looking at me."

"Sorry. Does that make you uneasy?"

"No, no," she quickly said. "I'm just not used to it. At least, not from a man like you."

Clint played up his wince as he asked, "Should I take that in a good way or a bad way?"

"It's good!" Realizing she'd been a little too anxious to say that, Ellie doubled her scrubbing on the largest platter and lowered her voice when she said, "It's good, Mr. Adams."

"Remember what I told you."

She grinned, but quickly tried to hide it. "I remember . . . Clint."

"That's better. So you really like Ned's work, huh?"

"Oh, yes. We were passing through there and Pa was being really difficult."

"So you decided to gouge him a little by making him plunk down his money for flowers and leaves glued to some paper?"

Ellie's cheeks reddened and she lowered her head. Judging by her expression, she wasn't ashamed of herself so much as she was trying to hide a wicked smile. "I liked those flowers. They're very pretty, but you may be right. Maybe a little."

"I don't see anything wrong with wanting a little something for yourself around here," Clint told her. "I don't see anything in this house that your father probably didn't pick out. Usually, there's a bit more of a woman's touch."

"There used to be." As she spoke those words, Ellie's voice tapered off and her eyes drifted toward the pictures that were framed and sitting on the mantel.

Spotting the kindly face of an older woman in several of those pictures, Clint put the pieces together quickly enough. "Your mother?" he asked.

Ellie nodded. "She's been gone a long while, but Pa never got past it. I don't want to push him. I don't think I could push him even if I wanted to."

Clint reached out to touch Ellie's arm. "It's good of you to stay with him. From what I've seen, you must have a bit of a saint in you to put up with him day in and day out."

"It's not too bad." Giggling under her breath, she added, "Maybe it is sometimes."

"Well, you'll have those pretty flowers to hang up soon enough," Clint told her as he dried off the platter and set it on the table with the other clean plates. "That should brighten things up."

Ellie dried her hands on the apron tied around her waist. Although she seemed meek with her head lowered, there was something else entirely when she raised it again. The little girl that was brought out by her father's presence was gone. Now, she looked to be every bit the young woman that she was. When Ellie looked at Clint, she had all the hunger in her eyes that any woman in her twenties might feel.

She stepped forward and placed her hands upon Clint's face, opening her mouth a bit as she lifted her lips to his. Clint reacted out of instinct. His hands went to her waist and he accepted the kiss she was giving him. Now that her body was pressed against him, she didn't remind him of a little girl at all. She was a woman through and through.

The moment she felt Clint's lips upon her own, Ellie sifted her fingers through his hair and pulled him closer. Letting out a soft, contented moan, she parted her lips and slipped her tongue into Clint's mouth just far enough for him to get a taste of her.

Clint was taken by surprise, mostly because he'd pegged Ellie wrong. He wasn't exactly disappointed or shocked, just surprised at how this quiet young lady could be so hungry for him.

Suddenly, she pulled back. Although the kiss was cut short, she was still close enough for him to feel the warmth of her breath as she said, "Oh, Lord. I . . . guess I got carried away. Was that too forward of me?"

"Forward?" Clint gulped. "Actually, it was the best dessert I could have asked for."

"You didn't exactly ask." Just then, Ellie's cheeks flushed as she felt Clint's erection through his jeans pushing against her body. Despite the fact that she was blushing, she didn't move away from him. Before she could say anything else, Clint moved in even closer.

This time, Clint wrapped one arm around her so he could encircle her waist. He kept the other on her hip simply because he liked the feel of her beneath her apron and simple dress. When he kissed her again, Clint could hear and even feel the contented purr that came from the back of her throat.

The kiss enveloped both of them so much that neither of them heard the gunshot right away.

A second later, Clint pulled back and looked around. "Did you hear that?"

Before Ellie could answer, another gunshot was fired. This one was followed by the booming sound of Hank's voice.

SEVENTEEN

"Who in the hell are you?" Hank shouted.

Acklund stepped forward. The .38 Smith and Wesson in his hand was still smoking. "You hiding a killer in there?"

To his credit, Hank didn't seem rattled in the least by the fact that a gun had been fired so recently. "Just stay put," he snarled. "When I come back out with my shotgun, I'm gonna blow your stinkin' head off!"

Hank made it halfway to his front door before Acklund fired again. This bullet whipped through the air to shatter the window to Hank's right. The older man paused with his hand outstretched. His head slowly turned toward the broken window and his voice rumbled from him like boiling water from a geyser. "You're payin' for that!"

"Just like you're gonna pay if you don't—"

"Let the old man go," Clint shouted from the shadows surrounding the house. After bolting through the door leading from the kitchen, he'd run around to get a look at who was causing all the commotion. Clint had his suspicions as soon as he'd left the house, but now he saw he was correct. "Your fight is with me."

Acklund snapped his head toward Clint while trying to cover the surprise on his face. He did a terrible job, but forced himself to smile arrogantly anyway. "You think we'd forget about you killing our brother?"

That choice of words made Clint nervous. The fact that Acklund had said "our" instead of "my" made him suspicious that the third man from the ambush was lurking about somewhere. Sure enough, Mose's blond hair stood out from one of the dark spots in the trees not too far away.

"Your brother died while trying to steal my horse," Clint pointed out. "He would have been strung up for such a thing no matter where he was caught. Besides, if you'd stuck around to see, you would have known that I didn't shoot him. He broke his own neck!"

"That don't matter!" Acklund said. "He'd still be alive if it weren't for you."

"You mean if I would have just let you men rob me?" Clint asked. "If you're expecting me to regret what happened, you'll be waiting a long time."

"Fine. No more waiting, then."

Clint had been hoping to put an end to the shooting to prevent Ellie or Hank from catching a stray bullet. He'd also hoped to keep Acklund talking long enough for any town law to come and check on the gunshots that had already been fired. The instant Clint saw the gleam in Acklund's eye, however, he knew it was too late for any of that. There would be more shots fired and he couldn't afford to wait around for anyone to help.

Clint reached for his Colt and cleared leather in a fraction of a second. He kept the gun at hip level so he could fire off a round without wasting time to aim. Acklund fired as well and both shots hissed through the air like a pair of angry wasps.

Acklund dropped, but Clint knew he hadn't been the one to put him on his back. Rather than fall over like a man that had been shot, Acklund fell to one knee so he could fire again. By the time Acklund got around to pulling his trigger, Clint was already on the move.

Knowing that Mose was still out there, Clint fired a shot in the last direction he'd seen the big blond man. He didn't hear a yelp of pain and didn't even hear a gunshot from that direction, which made Clint suspect Mose had already picked another spot. Clint fired another bullet toward the trees anyway, followed by another shot at Acklund to buy himself enough time to make it to some cover.

The only other thing on the porch was an old swing, so Clint ducked behind it and quickly replaced the spent rounds in his Colt with fresh bullets from his gun belt. Just as he was finished reloading, Clint heard the thunderous bang of the front door being kicked open.

"Clear off my property right now!" Hank roared as he fired a shotgun blast into the air.

"Get back in the house!" Clint hollered.

"The hell I will!" Hank replied before firing off his second barrel.

Since Clint couldn't see in the dark well enough to know if Hank had hit anything, he waited until the older man pulled the spent shell casings from his shotgun. Once Hank was busy with that, Clint rushed over to him and knocked him back into the house with his shoulder. Hank was still cussing up a storm when Clint stepped back outside and pulled the door shut behind him.

Another shot was fired from the shadows, but Clint couldn't get a look at who'd fired it. Both Acklund and Mose had retreated far enough into the trees that they couldn't be seen until they fired. The moment Clint saw another muzzle flash, he sighted in on it and returned fire. He followed that up with another quick shot that punched through one of the trees.

"You can't get us both!" Acklund shouted as he ran from the tree that had just been hit.

Clint was about to squeeze his trigger when he heard a twig snap to his immediate left. He turned to find Mose creeping up on him from that side. The blond man must have circled around the house to flank Clint from and damn near pulled his trick off before Clint turned and fired. The Colt bucked against Clint's hand, but Mose had already ducked back around the house. Splinters flew and Mose let out a pained moan.

"My damn eye!" Mose wailed.

"Now!" Acklund hollered. "Shoot the bastard!"

Now that he knew where both men were, Clint ran across the porch to put some distance between himself and both of the brothers. His eyes were becoming accustomed to the dark, so Clint was able to pick out Acklund's shape crouching against a tree. Clint aimed at that shape and fired, knowing that he'd probably missed.

With Clint away from the window, Acklund had to wait for his own eyes to adjust. Unlike Clint, however, he didn't seem too concerned with picking his shots or who else might get hit along the way. Standing up and hopping away from his tree to clear his line of fire, Acklund pointed his six-shooter at Clint and pulled the trigger as quickly as he could.

The .38 barked again and again, illuminating Acklund's face with a constant flow of sparks. When Clint's entire body whipped around with enough force to make him stagger against the side of the house, Acklund shouted, "I told you I'd get you, asshole! That was for Dave!"

Mose ran around the front of the house with his pistol held at the ready. Before he could get a clear shot at Clint, the front door came open again and Hank's shotgun erupted once more. Mose pulled himself away from the door so quickly that his feet kicked out from under him and his backside landed heavily against the porch.

Another shot cracked through the air as Acklund rushed toward his brother. That shot was soon answered by another blast from the shotgun, but both explosions were followed by the slap of hammers against spent shells.

"Shit!" both Acklund and Hank shouted at the same time.

Both men needed to reload, but Hank's shotgun would take a lot less time. The older man was spouting a steady stream of obscenities as he opened the shotgun, pulled out the empty shells, and struggled to get fresh ones in.

Mose had fought to get to his feet by now and had his gun pointed at Hank.

"Forget about him," Acklund said. "I already wounded that murdering asshole."

Mose grinned and lowered his pistol.

By the time Hank closed his shotgun and pulled back the hammers, he no longer had a target. He nearly emptied one barrel at the sound of another gunshot coming from the side of the house. The only thing he could hear after that were frantic footsteps racing into the night.

EIGHTEEN

As soon as Hank rounded the corner on the side of the house where Clint had last been seen, a shot was fired that nearly caused him to jump out of his britches. The sparks from the barrel blinded him for a few seconds and his ears were ringing louder than a set of church bells.

"For Christ's sake, it's just me!" the old man shouted.

Clint was leaning against the side of the house as if his shoulder were the only thing keeping him up. His mouth moved, but Hank was still unable to hear anything. Although he saw Hank rubbing his ears and straining to pick out something through the rest of the noise, Clint didn't lower his Colt.

"My fault," Clint grumbled as he squinted to get a look at the figures that had bolted into the shadows.

"What?" Hank asked.

"Never mind. Where'd they go?"

"Huh?"

Clint was prepared to shout even louder, but he could tell by the old man's features he still wouldn't be heard. Realizing he'd been the one to put the ringing in the old man's ears with that last wild shot, Clint wanted to let out a different sort of shout. Instead, he flipped open the cylinder of his Colt to replace the spent rounds.

The back door had squeaky hinges, which Clint heard now

as well as when he'd snuck out that way earlier. The footsteps that came his way were light and frantic, telling him there was no need to reload any faster or worry about who was coming toward him.

Just as Clint had expected, Ellie rushed around the house amid a series of panicked steps. "Oh, my God, Clint! They shot you!"

Clint held out a hand to silence her and angrily waved at Hank when the old man started to grunt for Ellie to repeat herself. Once they were quiet, Clint surveyed the surrounding area and strained his ears for any noises he could pick up.

The only movement came from the trees swaying in the wind.

The only sounds were rustling leaves.

Once Clint let out the breath he'd been holding, the other two took that as their cue to start up where they'd left off.

Ellie rushed over to him and grabbed Clint's arm. "You're shot, Clint. Does it hurt?"

"Who the blazes were those men?" Hank growled. "They knew you, sure as hell, so don't try to tell me any different."

His gun reloaded, Clint shoved it into its holster and immediately swore at the pain that movement caused. Ellie tried to grab at him and her father kept shuffling to stay directly in Clint's sights. Finally, Clint shoved past both of them and snapped, "I am shot! We need to get inside in case they try to take shots at us from the dark."

"But they're . . ." Hank protested.

"And you're . . ." Ellie added.

Before either of them could finish, Clint looked to Hank and said, "Yes. I have seen those men before and I knew they were after me." Looking at Ellie, he said, "And yes. I've been shot. It hurts, but it won't do any good to stay out here. Can we go back into the house now?"

Father and daughter both looked stunned. They blinked, looked at each other, and then nodded. Hank seemed to grudgingly agree, while Ellie was anxious to help Clint make the short journey back to the door. Clint let her hold onto his arm, since it allowed him to speed her up a bit in the process. Once the two of them got moving, Hank followed soon enough.

"Lock the doors," Clint said once they were inside. "Put something in front of them or do what you can to keep them shut. Close the windows. You have any curtains?"

"Some," Ellie replied.

"Close them. Is there any law in this town?" When he didn't get a response right away, Clint raised his voice. "Hank! Is there any law around here?"

"Some."

Clint wasn't sure if it was the two similar answers to such different questions or the dizziness that was creeping into his head from his fresh wound, but he couldn't help laughing.

"What's so damned funny?" Hank demanded. "We take care of ourselves just fine without bothering the deputy."

"What about the sheriff?"

Hank shook his head solemnly. "There's just a deputy. The sheriff went missing a few months back and . . ."

Suddenly, there was a series of tapping knocks against the front door. Ellie was gathering up some towels and water, which she almost dropped in her surprise at the sudden commotion.

"That's probably Cale now," Hank said. Looking at Clint, he explained. "Deputy Cale."

"Make certain before you open the door."

Hank waved off Clint's warning, but went to the window first before touching the door handle. After pulling back the curtain a bit, he peeked outside for a second. That was enough for him to step over to the door. "Told you so," he said over his shoulder.

Clint lowered himself onto a chair. Despite the pain shooting through his right arm, he kept that hand upon the grip of his Colt so he was ready to draw if things took a turn for the worse. Ellie approached him and dropped to her knees so she could get a better look at his arm.

"Let me see to that," she insisted.

"Just a second," Clint replied.

Hank opened the door and exchanged a few pleasantries

with the man outside. He then let a tall, spindly fellow into the house and closed the door again. Since there were no more gunshots and no one else trying to get inside, Clint let his hand fall away from his holster.

Part of him was glad the fight seemed to be over.

Another part was still steaming because of how the fight had ended.

NINETEEN

Deputy Cale was a good deal taller than Hank, but still looked to weigh at least sixty pounds lighter than the old man. In fact, the double-rig holster he wore even seemed to outweigh him. The two mismatched guns in that holster were obviously too big for the deputy's hands, but the lawman strutted into the house as if he were routing out the devil himself.

"I heard shooting," the deputy said.

"Most of the town must have heard it," Clint grumbled.

When Cale glared at Clint without getting any reaction in return, he shifted his eyes toward Hank, who at least gave him an annoyed shrug. "You mind telling me what the shooting was about?" Narrowing his eyes into what he must have thought was a menacing stare, Cale added, "Or maybe I should just take a look at your gun to see if it's been fired."

"You want to feel the barrel?" Clint snapped. "Sniff for burnt powder? How about I save you the trouble? I fired it at the two men who tried to ambush me and this family while you were off somewhere else waiting for the noise to die down before you got over here. In fact, this is the second time those two tried to shoot me, but I'm the one under suspicion!"

Despite the considerable weight of the two guns he carried, Deputy Cale seemed uncomfortable as he shifted on his feet. "I wouldn't know about the second time. Did it happen here in town?"

"This was the second," Clint said. "The first was on the way here."

"Oh," Cale said with relief. "Then I wouldn't know about that. What can you tell me about what happened just now?"

Before Clint could answer, he felt a pinch in his arm. With all that had happened and all he'd been trying to do to keep the wrong people from getting shot while also trying to put the right ones down, Clint hadn't had a chance to look at his wound. It was a messy spot on his arm, with enough blood to soak through his sleeve. The sleeve had also been shredded by the passing bullet, and Ellie had already cut the sleeve away.

The pinch Clint had just felt was Ellie's sewing needle, which she'd pulled through so she could get a length of thread to close his wound. She drizzled some more water on the wound to reveal a long, gaping cut that went straight across Clint's right elbow.

"Did that hurt?" she asked.

"Not too badly," Clint said through gritted teeth. "How bad is the wound?"

"I can't see any bone—"

"Oh, Lord," Cale groaned.

Glancing nervously between the deputy and Clint, Ellie continued, "But there's a pretty deep cut. There might have been a chip taken from your elbow when it passed."

Cale straightened up and placed his hands upon his hips.

"Can you bend it?" she asked.

Without hesitation, Clint lifted his arm and bent it. The thread dangled from his flesh, but there weren't any real stitches to tear. Even so, Clint felt as if he were ripping his arm off when he bent it past a certain point. "Hurts, but I can use it."

"Do you . . . feel anything in there?" Ellie asked.

Cale pulled in a breath as the color drained from his face.

Clint shook his head. "There's definitely no bullet in there."

"Are you sure?"

"I've been shot enough to know. It feels more like a bad cut."

Ellie reached out, placed her fingertips on either side of the wound, and eased it open.

"Holy . . ." Cale moaned as he turned around and leaned against Hank for support.

The older man immediately shoved the lawman's hand away. "You come here to whine or are you goin' after them gunmen?" he asked.

"Was . . . uhh . . . was this gentleman an offending party?" Cale stammered. "I mean . . . uhh . . . do you want me to—"

"He didn't start it, if that's what you mean," Hank snapped. "He stepped in to help."

"Then I'll go see if I can find where those men went." Before he made it more than a couple of steps toward the door, Cale turned and asked, "Do any of you know where they went?"

Clint, Ellie, and Hank all shook their heads.

"All right, then," the deputy said. "I'll look and ask about and come back later."

Even before the door had fully closed behind the lawman, Hank grumbled, "Good riddance."

Clint couldn't agree more. Rather than say as much, he looked down to watch Ellie stitch his elbow. "I appreciate the help. You need me to do anything?"

"Just sit still," she replied. "I used to lend a hand to Doc Ackermon when he was in town, so I can do stitches well enough."

Hank stomped over to Clint's side, crossed his arms, and glared down at him. "You gonna live?"

"Not indefinitely," Clint replied, "but this scratch won't be the end of me."

"Good, then you can tell me what in the hell that was all about!"

Before Clint could say anything to that, Ellie turned to her father and told him, "Can't you wait for a bit? He's hurt and he got that way by saving both of us!"

Clint looked at Hank, but didn't need to say a word. Judging by the sheepish look on the old man's face, Ellie's words had been enough.

"I suppose you're right," Hank muttered. "I still wanna know why them boys were after you. The least you can do is let us know if they'll be comin' back or not."

"To be honest," Clint said, "I'm not quite sure. The last I saw of them, Acklund was charging around the house after I was picking myself up."

"Acklund?" Hank asked.

"The one with the darker hair. As soon as I caught sight of him, I fired a shot. At least, I thought I did. I'd just gotten hit and things were a little muddled for a second or two," Clint admitted.

"Well, I saw 'em both take off runnin'," Hank told him. "They was either scared or riled up because they moved like their tails was on fire."

Clint thought it over for a second or two, but didn't come up with much. "It would be good if they just thought I was killed. That way, we wouldn't see them again. Of course, that doesn't sit well with me."

"Why?" Ellie asked.

Clint's eyes narrowed to intense slits and he said, "Because I wouldn't see them again. Those men tried to rob me on my way into town. They had another one with them that turned out to be their brother. He was killed while they tried to ambush me."

"You shot him?" Hank asked.

"No, he tried to steal my horse and broke his neck along the way."

"Serves him right, then."

Clint nodded. "I agree, but they're not exactly of the same mind on the subject. Since their brother was killed and they think I did it, I suppose there's no question they'll be back. There's the off chance that they got a quick look at me and thought I was bleeding from a worse spot than my elbow, but I don't want to gamble on that and put you folks or this house at risk. I should probably get away from here."

Ellie placed her hand on Clint's shoulder as if she thought he intended on riding away at that very instant. "You won't go anywhere. Not until this wound is properly stitched."

"They found me once after I thought I'd shaken free of them," Clint said. "That means they're better trackers than I thought or just plain lucky. Either way, they know where I am. If I stay here, it'd just be asking for trouble."

"Then stay at Aunt Iris's!" Ellie said as her eyes snapped open wide.

In contrast to his daughter, Hank furrowed his brow until his eyes were almost closed. "Shut your mouth, girl! That ain't your place to do with as you please."

"She left it to both of us, Pa," Ellie insisted. "And she would have wanted it to be used to help a good man like Clint." Seeing that her father wasn't quick to agree, she added, "A good man who saved our lives."

"All right, all right," Hank said as he waved his arms. "No need to keep sticking my nose in it! He can stay there, but I'll be the one who takes him and you'll steer clear."

"I need to finish dressing his wound," Ellie said.

"Then finish it here."

"I'll need to check on it and clean it."

Hank rolled his eyes, recognizing a losing battle when he heard one. "Good Lord Almighty!"

Ellie smiled and patted Clint's shoulder, knowing better than to spoil a victory with any more negotiations.

TWENTY

Aunt Iris had lived on the south side of town in a little cottage that still smelled like dried flowers. The moment he stepped inside, Clint looked at the walls for anything in a frame that might have also come from Ned's barbershop. There were a few little paintings of roses here and there, which weren't quite good enough to be done by an artist. The cottage only had one large room with another smaller one just off the kitchen. Once Ellie had lit the lantern next to the door, Clint could see the frame of a bed that took up most of the smaller room.

"If your father gives you too much trouble about that picture," he said, "you could always hang it up here."

Ellie looked around as well, which brought a smile to her face. "That's part of why I liked it so much. All those flowers remind me of her." She kept her hand on Clint as if he were about to fall over any second. Once they were both inside, she closed the door but didn't stray too far from it. Keeping her ear pressed to the dusty wood, she whispered, "You think those men will come back?"

"Not for a while. I doubt they even know where we are."

Shifting her eyes toward him, Ellie cautiously asked, "Isn't that what you thought when they attacked you the last time?"

"Yes, but I wasn't watching for them last time. They scampered off like scalded dogs, so I thought that was the end of it. Now I know better. I kept my eyes and ears open every step of the way between your house and this one."

She nodded. "I didn't mean to nag."

"I know. You actually made a good point. I got careless the first time I met up with those men, plain and simple."

"And what about this time?" Ellie asked as she eyed Clint's bandaged elbow.

"This time they got lucky," he told her with a bit of an edge to his voice. "They picked good spots and waited until dark. If they were better shots, they would have finished us all off."

"Oh."

The distress was plain enough to see in Ellie's eyes. She was also growing a little pale and made her way to one of the chairs around a small dining table. There was another larger chair against the nearby wall, but it was blocked by a basket full of knitting supplies on one side and a footstool directly in front of it.

Clint settled into the chair next to Ellie at the table. She'd placed her hand on top of the table, so he covered it with his own. "That's not to say this situation is hopeless," he assured her.

That kindled a bit of a spark in her eyes, but not a very big one. "Really?"

"There are marksmen out there who could kill you with one shot without you ever knowing they were there. That doesn't mean you should worry yourself to death about them."

"Uhh . . . I guess not."

"There are also plenty of ways for a horse to knock the stuffing out of you. Do you worry yourself about that?"

"No," she said definitively.

"You can't spend your life worrying about any of that. There are plenty more loudmouth idiots like those two that ruined our supper tonight than there are real assassins. The truth is you've got to be a certain kind of someone to get one of those assassins after you. Riling up loudmouthed idiots isn't that hard."

Ellie forced a shaky smile onto her face. "I guess so."

"Those men aren't after you and they're not after your father. They're after me and now that I know they weren't scared away that first time, I can watch out for them. They won't get a chance to ambush me again. I'll see to that."

"It sounds like you've had killers after you before. Is that why you carry that gun with you all the time?"

Clint instinctively reached for the modified Colt, but felt pain from his wound lance all the way to his fingertips and up to his shoulder. Even though the pistol was right where it should be, the gun felt awfully far away. "A lot of men carry guns," he replied.

"But most of those are loudmouthed idiots or gunfighters. You don't strike me as the former, so you must be the latter."

"You ever think there may be more than two choices?"

"Sure there are, but you definitely strike me as the latter. Tell me different."

"I'm not a gunfighter," Clint told her. Even though she let the matter drop, he could tell Ellie didn't quite believe him.

TWENTY-ONE

Ellie's stitches held up pretty well. Clint put them to the test after she'd curled up and fallen asleep in the big old chair surrounded by knitting needles.

Clint stood in the section of the room closer to the dining table, which also gave him a clear view through the cottage's wide windows. The window directly in front of him looked out onto the main street, which led straight through town. To his right, there was a large garden, which was open enough for him to spot anyone approaching the cottage from that direction. The window behind him was narrow, but looked out onto a porch that wasn't much bigger than the dining table. Clint had gone out there to test the boards and found the porch to be more than squeaky enough to suit his needs. The windows to his left looked out to the neighboring cottage, which was so close that only a cat could squeeze between it and this cottage.

Nobody would be sneaking up on the place. Clint was certain of that much.

After assuring Ellie she was safe, Clint urged her to get some sleep. Actually, he'd insisted she go home, but she wasn't having any of that. Since she wanted to stay with him and make certain he didn't rip his stitches, she planted herself at his side and wasn't about to budge. Finally, she'd gone to sit in the big chair and even picked up the knitting needles to do some work. Her hands moved so quickly that Clint became convinced she spent plenty of time in this cottage. Considering her father's sour disposition, he didn't blame her.

Before long, Ellie's breathing had become deeper and her head had fallen forward. Clint made sure she was comfortable, wrapping an afghan around her so she would stay warm. Then he took a position where he could see outside in every direction. Once there, he extinguished the lantern and stood in the dark until his eyes adjusted to the shadows. After that happened, the light from the moon and stars was enough to give him a good look at the street and garden.

Clint stood and moved his arm in a slow circle. His elbow felt as if it had been dipped in kerosene and lit by a match, but it still bent just fine. When he felt the first trace of blood trickling beneath his bandage, Clint removed his shirt and unwrapped the bandage around his elbow.

Now that his elbow had been cleaned up a bit, the wound didn't look so bad. Of course, being closed up by stitches helped. The wound itself looked more like a tear in his flesh. The edges were as ragged as ripped parchment, held together by thread. Flexing his arm a few times, Clint watched as the wound shifted with every movement. The blood that had come out was barely a trickle and was already drying up.

He lowered his arm, made a fist, and glanced at the windows. There was nobody outside. In fact, it was late enough that even the rowdy echoes from the saloon had faded away. The street was just as still as the garden, which made even the occasional nocturnal critters easy to spot.

The more he moved his arm, the easier it became. Now that he'd seen the wound up close, Clint tested himself a bit further. He reached for the Colt, took hold of it, and pulled it from its holster. His grip slipped a little, which caused the end of the barrel to snag upon the edge of the holster.

Clint dropped the weapon back in place and drew again. The movement was smooth, but not as fast as he would have liked. He tried again, speeding himself up to something closer to his normal pace. The weapon came up freely, so he tried again.

If Clint's life had been on the line against someone who knew what they were doing, he knew he would be in trouble. Against the two men who insisted on coming after him, however, he put his odds at well above average.

Just for the hell of it, Clint holstered the Colt and allowed his arm to hang normally. He took a few breaths, imagined he'd spotted someone through the window, and then went for his Colt as if he intended on pulling the trigger.

Pain shot through his arm in mid-draw, tripping him up before he cleared leather. Clint swore under his breath and replaced the gun.

"You shouldn't be doing that," Ellie said. "Not yet anyway."

Clint looked over at her and grinned. "Just seeing where I stand."

"You're standing in front of open windows. Didn't you say that was bad?"

"Bad for you and your father," he told her. "I wouldn't mind it if those two decided to stick their necks out and give me a clear shot for a change."

Ellie winced as if she were the one who'd been wounded. "You are a gunfighter. I knew it."

"Just because I carry a gun doesn't make me a gunfighter."

"Is that a bad thing? Being a gunfighter, I mean?"

"Not as such," Clint admitted. "Most folks just think of gunfighters as killers and murderers. Gunfighters sell their trigger fingers to the highest bidder or shoot men for the pleasure of it. I just go about my business and do what needs to be done. I don't know what you'd call that, but gunfighter doesn't seem to suit it."

"Neither does flower courier," she said with a chuckle.

Clint laughed a bit, too. "What about protector of fine arts?"

"No," she said as she moved closer to him. "Not that, either. I'll have to come up with something more suitable before you heal up."

"I'm doing well enough. Since those two haven't made another play at me, I think they're off somewhere licking their wounds. I'll head back to the room I rented once there are more people about. That way, plenty of folks will see where I am. If those two idiots are still in town, they'll see it, too."

"But you can't just go away," Ellie said. "You're hurt."

"It's nothing. I can still hold my gun." Seeing the critical look in her eyes, Clint added, "I can hold it good enough to go up against them."

"And what if those stitches tear and you can hardly move your arm?"

"Then I'll draw with my left. It's not as fast as the right, but it's good enough. You and your father were almost shot tonight," Clint told her as he grabbed her by both arms and stared at her so she knew he meant business. "You stay around me too long and those idiots will get the wrong idea. They might even try getting to you so they can get to me. The quicker I get away from you, the better.

"Those bushwhackers have always gone for the easy shots. They'll wait until I'm alone or until they can get the drop on me. I'm not about to hide in a crowd," Clint said, "but I won't let them get the drop on me again either. You don't want to be around if they decide to take another run at me."

Ellie's face took on a darkness that had nothing to do with the lantern cooling on its hook. "You're not going anywhere tonight, Clint. I'll see to that."

Clint glanced at the window that faced east. "You've been asleep for a while, Ellie. There isn't much left of tonight."

"Fine," she said as she pulled the string that kept the front of her dress laced up. "Then I guess we'll just have to make the best of the time we have."

TWENTY-TWO

Ellie's dress came off like water running down her body, pooling at her feet. Stepping out of the bundle of clothing, she wrapped her arms around Clint's body and pressed her nakedness against him. The moment she felt his hands upon her waist, she let out a slow, contented sigh.

"I want you, Clint. I want you so bad."

"Maybe we should get away from all these windows."

Suddenly, every muscle in Ellie's body tensed. It felt awfully good from Clint's side, but she obviously wasn't so comfortable since all of her clothes were piled up at her feet. Rather than wait for her to regain her composure, Clint picked Ellie up and carried her in his arms to the only other room in the cottage.

She wrapped her arms around his neck and swung her legs during the short ride.

Clint stepped through the narrow door, finding that the room was just as small as it had looked when he'd peeked inside earlier. The bed wasn't large, but it took up most of the space within the closet-sized area. Other than the bed, there was only an oval mirror hanging on the wall.

"You said this was your aunt's house?" Clint asked.

"She didn't live here for years before she passed on," Ellie told him.

"And where did she pass?"

"At another of my aunt's places in Illinois."

"All right," Clint said as he put Ellie down onto the bed. "Just making sure."

Quickly positioning herself so she was on her knees at the edge of the mattress, Ellie pulled at Clint's buttons as if he weren't doing it fast enough. "Don't worry about a thing, Clint. Nobody comes here anymore."

"And your father? He knows we're here."

"He must already be asleep. It'd take a hell of a lot more than gunshots to pry that old man from his pillow."

By this time, Clint's shirt had been ripped off, his gun belt had been set aside, and his jeans were being pulled down. After kicking off his boots and taking a good look at Ellie, Clint didn't want to discuss anything else.

Her hair looked dark red in the shadows and her skin looked even paler in the moonlight that trickled through the small, plate-sized square of a window. Her breasts fit perfectly in Clint's hands and she trembled when he cupped them. She moaned louder when he rolled her nipple between his thumb and forefinger. As the soft, pink skin became taut, Ellie's left hand wandered along the front of her body and then worked its way down. When her fingers drifted through the soft downy hair between her legs, her eyes snapped open and she looked ready to blush again.

"I didn't think," she said in a hurry. "I was just . . ."

"That's all right," Clint assured her as he placed his hand over hers. "From here it looks just fine."

Ellie kept her eyes open and slowly moved her hand between her legs. Before long, Clint urged her to rub even faster and she let her head drop back. Her legs opened a bit more and she moaned softly as Clint's hands ran up and down the tips of her pussy. Just as her legs were starting to shake, Ellie felt something else between her legs.

Clint eased forward until the tip of his cock brushed against her hand. When she looked down to see his hand was no longer between her legs, Ellie pulled in a quick breath. Rather than pump any further, Clint reached down to scoop both hands under Ellie's backside. From there, he lifted her up a bit and pulled her toward the edge of the bed. As she was brought forward, Clint moved into her.

"Oh . . . oh my," she stammered.

Her pussy was tight around him and her entire body trembled. Clint could tell by the look in her eyes that her trembling was due to pleasure rather than nervousness. He smiled down at Ellie and gently eased in and out of her.

As she became wetter, Ellie was able to lie back and enjoy what Clint was doing. After spreading her legs open wide and reaching down to rub herself as he pumped back and forth, Ellie began to breathe quicker in expectation of an oncoming climax. Even though she'd braced herself for it, her orgasm still took her by surprise.

Ellie arched her back and reached out with her free hand to grip the blankets on top of the bed. Short, gasping moans came out of her as she bucked and wriggled on the bed.

Clint enjoyed watching her for a few seconds, but then he reached down to place his hands upon her chest. Rubbing her nipples against his palms, he waited until her orgasm had subsided before pumping into her even harder. Ellie's thighs were slick with her own moisture, so she took every inch of him without a problem.

When she opened her eyes, it was as though she were just waking from a very good dream. She reached between her legs again, slipped her fingers on either side of Clint's shaft, and rubbed up and down. "You like that?" she asked.

Clint leaned his head back to savor what she was doing to him. "Yeah. I sure do."

"I want it harder," she said.

Feeling Ellie's fingers on him while he was inside of her made him as hard as he could get, but Clint was pretty sure she wasn't talking about that. He leaned forward as Ellie lifted her legs so her ankles were resting upon his shoulders. Grabbing onto both legs just above the knee, Clint thrust into her with a little more force.

"Yes, Clint. Harder."

Clint pumped into her harder.

"Oh, God! Like that!"

Clint tightened his grip on her legs and pounded between her legs. Ellie grabbed onto the bed and begged him to keep going. Soon, she couldn't even make a sound because her entire body was gripped in a climax that caused all of her muscles to jump beneath her skin. Entering her while her pussy gripped onto him that way was more than enough to push Clint past his limit. One more thrust, and he exploded inside of her.

"Good . . . good Lord," Ellie gasped. "I've never felt so good."

"Just wait," Clint replied. "We've still got plenty of time until morning."

TWENTY-THREE

The sun was barely up high enough to smear its light upon the lowest clouds. It was a crisp morning and the air was still cold enough to turn every one of Hank Mason's breaths into steam. His hands were stuffed into his pockets and the collar of his jacket was raised so it could cover a good portion of his neck. When he spotted a familiar face while hurrying down the street, Hank nodded quickly rather than return the wave he was given.

"Mornin', Hank," a storekeeper said as he swept his front stoop.

"Yeah." Hank grunted.

A butcher carried a ham hock on his shoulder from the wagon that had brought it into town. "Cold day, huh Hank?"

"Yeah."

Someone else asked about the state of the mill, but Hank didn't even respond to them. He was close enough to see his destination, so he hurried there without dawdling for so much as a second. By the time he got to the front door of Iris's cottage, he'd built up almost enough steam to crash through the door without opening it.

Hank reached out with both hands. One hand grabbed the door handle and the other stuck his key into the lock. Both hands worked together so he turned the key a fraction of a second before shoving the door open. After yanking the key out and stuffing it into his pocket, he rapped his knuckles upon the door a few times.

"You still here, Adams?" Hank bellowed. "Ellie? Where the hell are you? You'd better not be . . ."

Having only taken a few steps into the cottage, Hank stood in front of the open door with the dining table to his left and the knitting chair to his right. Directly in front of him was the narrow door leading into the bedroom. What Hank saw through the door took the breath from his lungs and lit a fire in his belly that showed as an inferno in his eyes.

Clint was lying upon the bed. Hank could just see his upper body, but that was enough to tell him that Clint was undressed. He could see the same applied to Ellie, since she was on top of Clint, supporting herself with both hands against his chest. If Hank had any doubt about what they were doing, they were erased by the expression of wide-eyed terror Ellie wore when she looked back at Hank.

"What are you doing here, Pa?" she screamed as she hopped off Clint and raced around the bed.

Hank stood where he was. His arms were frozen where they'd been when he'd stopped walking. Even his legs were partially bent as if he were a statue that was supposed to be moving instead of a man who couldn't. Even though he'd changed Ellie's linens since she was a baby, seeing her bare bottom as she ran to gather her clothes wasn't a welcome sight.

"Why didn't you knock?" Ellie shouted. "What are you doing here?"

Clint rolled out of bed so his back was to the door. He picked up his clothes as well, but wasn't doing it nearly fast enough for Hank's liking.

As Ellie peeked through the door again, Hank finally found the strength to move again. Ellie shouted and may have even started crying, but Hank didn't care about any of that. All he wanted to do was get out of that cottage as quickly as his legs would carry him.

TWENTY-FOUR

"Oh, no! Oh, no! Oh, no!"

Clint pulled his jeans on and shrugged into his shirt, hoping Ellie would settle down a little when he was done. Even as he buckled on his gun belt, she was still fretting with the laces on her dress and muttering those same words again and again.

"It's all right," Clint said as he placed his hand upon her shoulder. "He's gone now."

That didn't help matters in the least. In fact, she seemed to boil over even more when she felt his hand upon her. Pulling away as if Clint were burning her, Ellie rushed out of the bedroom. Her arms were crossed and she huddled down as if she were afraid of knocking her head against a low beam. "It doesn't matter if he's gone. He saw us!"

"Yeah, well . . ."

Wheeling around, she shouted, "How can you be so calm?"

"It was embarrassing, that's for certain. I'm not exactly happy to be found that way either. Come to think of it, how about I just have that picture sent over to your house when it's ready? That way—"

Clint couldn't see Ellie at the moment, but he could hear her crying in the next room. He followed the sounds all the way to the large chair that was surrounded by knitting supplies. "It's embarrassing, but it's not worth all of this," he said.

"You don't understand," she said from behind both hands.

Clint looked around the cottage until he found what he was looking for. Walking over to where his boots had been dropped, he collected them and then pulled one of the dining chairs over to where Ellie was sitting. "He's not my father, but I sort of know what you're talking about. When I was a boy, someone once found me while—"

"It's not like that," Ellie snapped. "Boys get away with murder, but girls aren't expected to do anything."

"Your father doesn't hit you, does he?"

When Ellie looked up at him, her tear-streaked face seemed even more appalled than it had before. "No! Pa loves me!"

"All right, then. He's also not stupid, so he must know you've been around men before. I mean," he added while pulling on one boot, "you're not a virgin. We both know that."

Ellie lowered her head. "We know that . . . but he doesn't."

Stopping with his other leg extended and his second boot halfway on, Clint asked, "He doesn't?"

"What do you think I should have done? Gone up to Pa after I met Bobby Hayes in his barn, tugged Pa on the sleeve, and told him why I snuck out that night?"

"No, I guess not."

"Or maybe I should have buttered him up with a good meal before I told him what Bobby did to his little girl that night and that I intended on going back for more helpings every night that summer!"

"Okay," Clint said. "I see your point. Fathers are different with their daughters than with their sons. I knew that already."

"Then why are you asking such stupid questions?"

Despite the fire in Ellie's voice and tone, Clint had to chuckle as he admitted, "Because I just don't see how this is the end of the world. It's embarrassing, but not long ago there were men shooting at all three of us. We could have been murdered, or even caught a stray bullet and died just the same."

Ellie's expression shifted from angry back to terror. "We could have?"

Clint shook his head and waved his hands as if he hoped he could literally clear the slate and start fresh. "No . . . what I meant was there was real danger and we could have gotten hurt. This is just embarrassing, Ellie. There's a big difference. Can't you see that?"

Ellie spent the next several seconds frantically wiping at the tears streaming from her eyes. Before too long, the tears stopped coming. "You . . . you're right." She sniffled.

Clint took a handkerchief from his pocket and handed it over to her. "At least nobody's shooting at us, right?"

She nodded and used Clint's handkerchief to dab at her eyes.

"And you've got to admit we had ourselves one hell of a time last night."

Finally, Ellie smiled. "And . . . and this morning, too."

"And this morning," Clint agreed. "There, now. You feel better?"

Just as she began to nod, Ellie jumped from her chair as the front door was kicked in and an armed man stomped inside. She let out a little yelp and raced to get behind Clint.

The sudden noise put Clint on the defensive and he swept one arm out to get Ellie behind him. His other hand went for the Colt at his side. Pain gnawed into his elbow from the wound and the stitches, but he managed to get to his pistol just fine. He stopped short of clearing leather, however, once he got a look at who'd come into the cottage.

"Hank?" Clint asked.

The older man glared at Clint as if he were a blood enemy. He held his shotgun at hip level, but raised it slowly as he replied, "You know damn well who I am. I'm that little girl's father."

"Pa!"

"Stand aside, Ellie girl," Hank warned. "This don't concern you."

To Clint's surprise, Ellie actually fought to get around him so she could face her father head-on. "It most certainly does concern me. I'm not a girl anymore! I'm a grown woman!"

Hank barely even seemed to realize that she was there. Instead, his eyes were fixed upon Clint as he growled, "And he's a grown man. I won't have him doing . . . doing what he done to you!"

Clint pushed Ellie behind him again and held his gun hand well away from his holster. "Look, Hank. This is awkward enough, but I didn't do anything to Ellie that she didn't—"

"I saw what you done, goddammit!"

"I know and I'm sorry," Clint said. "Maybe I should just leave."

"You ain't goin' nowhere, mister. That is unless you take my girl along with you. Once you're married, you can live wherever you please."

TWENTY-FIVE

Every muscle in Clint's gun arm wanted to draw his pistol.

Every instinct in Clint's head told him to draw the pistol.

The longer he looked down the wrong end of that shotgun, the harder it got for him to leave the modified Colt where it was.

"Look here, Hank," Clint said in a voice that was just as steady as his arm. "You're making a mistake."

"The hell I am," Hank snarled. "You made the mistake when you bedded my daughter like she was some kind of—"

"Stop right there!" Ellie said.

Hank blinked as if he'd just now realized she was in the same room. "I told you to step aside, girl."

"Why? So you can shoot Clint? So you can kill the man who saved both of our lives?"

"If he saved you just so he could get you alone, then yeah," Hank replied. "I would shoot that man."

Clint had looked into the eyes of many killers in his day. He'd stared down the barrels of more guns than he could count, which gave him a good handle on judging the men holding those guns. Playing poker for almost as long helped him figure out when a man was bluffing. All of those things combined to tell Clint he had a definite problem with Hank Mason.

The shotgun was steady in Hank's hands and his finger was curled expectantly around the trigger.

The tone in Hank's voice was an even snarl and didn't falter in the slightest when he'd made that last threat.

Hank wasn't bluffing. Clint would stake his life on that much.

The only thing that remained was what Clint would do about it.

"I don't want to hurt you, Hank," Clint said.

One corner of Hank's mouth curled into a grin. "I'm not the one that's about to be hurt here, boy. Even if you can get to that fancy gun of yours, I'll be able to cut you down."

Clint knew better than that, but there was no need to push it. Instead, he gave Hank what he wanted by putting a more concerned expression on his face when he asked, "What do you want from me?"

"You heard me the first time. You're gonna marry my daughter."

"Are you serious?"

"Why?" Hank asked as his eyes narrowed. "You'll fuck her, but you won't marry her?"

"That's enough, Pa!" Ellie shouted as she stomped forward despite the shotgun in her father's hands.

"He just called you a whore!" Hank said.

"He did no such thing! You're the one who said that word and it makes me sick that you did!"

For the first time since he'd stormed into the cottage, Hank's anger dimmed a bit. He looked at his daughter, but couldn't do so for long before shifting his eyes back to Clint. Lowering his voice as if Ellie somehow wouldn't hear him, he said, "You treated her like one, you son of a bitch, and I won't have anyone treating my daughter that way."

"He didn't, Pa. It was—"

Before she could get into any unnecessary details, Clint extended his arm so she couldn't walk any farther. Fortunately, Ellie stopped talking when she bumped against Clint's arm.

"If you have a problem with me, let's hear it," Clint said.

"You know my goddamn problem with you!" Hank bellowed.

"Fine. Then put the gun down."

Hank didn't move.

Locking his eyes on Hank, Clint took half a step forward like he was the predator stalking its prey. "Only a stupid kid aims a gun at another man to look tough. Someone your age should know better than that. If you intend on spilling blood, then you'd best be ready to spill some of your own."

Hank still didn't move, but Clint could see the wheels turning behind the man's eyes.

"Lower that shotgun so we can settle this like men," Clint said. "My offer stands to leave if that's what you want. Or you could take a swing at me if you're still of a mind to hurt me. This has already gone too far, so don't push it any further."

Ellie nodded vigorously. "Yes, Pa. For my sake. I don't want to see you shot or killed. I don't want either of you shot."

Letting out a slow breath, Hank relaxed his finger on the trigger. "You first, Adams."

"We'll lower our guns together," Clint offered. When he saw Hank nod, Clint slowly began to unfasten his gun belt. He didn't pull the strap out all the way until he saw Hank following through on his own part of the bargain. Even though Hank was lowering his shotgun, Clint said, "Why doesn't Ellie collect both our guns?"

"All right," Ellie said before her father could refuse. "That's fair." She went over to her father first and held out her hand. "Give me the shotgun, Pa."

Reluctantly, Hank complied. He didn't actually let go of the shotgun, however, until he saw Clint removing the gun belt from around his waist and holding it out toward his daughter.

Ellie held the shotgun by the barrel and turned toward Clint. Since he was going to have to be true to his word if he was going to get out of this situation, Clint handed over his gun belt.

"There," Clint said. "Happy?"

Hank lowered his head and took a step forward. He then

leaned into a swing so his fist made it all the way to Clint's chin. The punch was fast, but Clint had seen it coming. Even so, he stood his ground and took it in the name of defusing the old man's temper.

The old man packed a wallop. Clint rubbed his jaw and blinked a few times. "Ellie, why don't you take those guns back to your house so your father and I can have a discussion?"

She wasn't anxious to leave the two alone, but Ellie nodded and carried the weapons out.

Clint watched her carefully to make certain Hank didn't make a desperate grab for his shotgun. He only lost sight of the old man for a second or two, but that was enough time for Hank to get his hands on something heavy and smash it against the back of Clint's head.

"Now I'm happy," Hank said as Clint slipped into unconsciousness.

TWENTY-SIX

Clint didn't know how long he was awake before he realized he could open his eyes. His head hurt so much that it felt as if his skull had been cracked and fire was leaking out. He figured it was a nasty dream, complete with ghostly voices that echoed through his ears without him being able to understand what they were saying.

After a while, Clint realized it was no dream.

The voices belonged to Hank and Ellie.

The pain was all too real.

So were the ropes wrapped tightly around his wrists and ankles.

Opening his eyes made Clint feel as if he were prying them open with a set of hot pokers. There wasn't much light in the room, but what little there was burned all the way through to the back of his skull. Clint closed his eyes, gritted his teeth, and braced himself for his next attempt.

This time, Clint opened his eyes and lifted his head. The pain that shot through him only added fuel to his fire. For a moment, he thought he could build up enough strength to bust out of his ropes. He even tried testing the ropes, but soon realized he was overstepping his limits. His ankles ached within his boots, and his wrists were cut open before he gave up and slumped back against the wall.

Unwilling to rest, Clint took in his surroundings while his body remained still. It only took him a second to realize he was still in Aunt Iris's cottage. In fact, he was in the same bedroom where he and Ellie had done the deed that had gotten Hank so riled up in the first place. The only reason he hadn't recognized it even sooner was because he was trussed up with his back to the door that led out to the main room. All he could see was the wall directly in front of him and the square window covered by thin curtains with red flowers stitched into them. It had been those god-awful curtains that had tipped Clint off.

Although Clint's arms and legs were tied up, there was nothing around his mouth. He pulled in a deep breath and was about to let out a holler when the door behind him was opened and a series of quick steps tapped over to him.

"Oh, Clint, you're all right," Ellie said. "Thank God."

Clint shifted his eyes to look at her, which hurt a lot more than it should have. "Ellie, get me out of here. Right now."

Dropping her voice to a whisper, she said, "I can't. Not while my pa's around."

"I don't care where your pa is," Clint snarled through gritted teeth. "Get these ropes off me because if I have to tear my way out of here, it's gonna be ugly."

Her face became even more distressed and her eyes immediately became red around the edges. "Please don't say that, Clint. You wouldn't really hurt us."

"Hank broke something over my head! He's holding me prisoner. If you won't let me go, that means you're an accomplice in this whole mess."

"If I let you go, you'll hurt Pa," Ellie whined.

"No. I won't." Even though Clint knew he had to be convincing, he was too angry to pull it off. There was too much heat in his blood for him to keep it from showing in his eyes. Still, he fought as hard as he could to do better on his second attempt. "I never wanted to hurt your father, Ellie. I was the one who tried to talk to him, remember? I didn't even make a move when he punched me."

"That's because you knew you had it comin'!" Hank shouted from the next room.

Once again, Clint did his damndest to keep from looking like he wanted to murder the old man. "I was willing to let the matter drop," Clint said loudly enough to be heard throughout the cottage.

"I just bet you was," Hank shouted back.

"Why don't you come in here and talk to me like a man?"

Not long after making that challenge, Clint heard heavy steps thumping toward him. Soon, the old man stepped into Clint's view, cradling the shotgun in one arm.

"What are you going to do, Hank?" Clint asked. "Drag a preacher into this room so he can perform a ceremony while I'm tied up?"

"Maybe. The preacher's an old fishin' buddy of mine. He's known Ellie since she was knee high to a grasshopper and I don't think he'd take any better to what you done than I did."

"Uncle Mike wouldn't approve of this and you know it," Ellie said.

"Uncle Mike nearly killed that boy that tried to get you into his barn that summer. You know that?"

Even Clint knew more of the story where that was concerned. Since neither one of them wanted to tell Hank the rest of it, Ellie shut her mouth and backed away.

"You've got to see this is crazy," Clint told him. "I know you must be upset, but this is taking it too far."

Hank looked down at him without showing a hint of emotion in his face. He cradled his shotgun like a baby and let his eyes wander as if to pick out the best target. When he glanced over at Ellie, the slightest hint of distaste drifted beneath his expression.

"You seem like a good sort, Clint," Hank admitted. "You did pull our fat from the fire the other night. If I untie you, will you stay put and wait for the preacher to get here?"

"Sure," Clint said.

Hank paused for a few seconds, leaned down, and said, "You'll run like a jackrabbit as soon as you get the chance.

Cool yer heels here for a bit more until you get enough sense to do the right thing."

Clint had plenty of opinions about the old man, but he had to admit one thing: Hank was probably deadly at poker.

TWENTY-SEVEN

During the time they'd spent together, before he was knocked out, Clint had told Ellie he'd rented a room at Bernadette's Room and Board. After Ellie saw her father leave the bedroom, she checked to make sure Clint was in one piece. Then she excused herself and joined her father in the large front room.

"Keep your mouth shut about this," Hank demanded. "The whole damn town don't need to know our affairs."

"I will as long as you don't hurt him while I'm gone," she replied. "He may be a prisoner, but he should have his things and some fresh clothes."

"Just so long as your man don't step out of line."

She stopped and spun around on her heel so she could storm back to where Hank was sitting. Once Ellie was at the table, she placed her hands on her hips and said, "If you hurt him, you'll never see me again."

It was the only real threat she could think of, but it seemed to do the trick. Hank scowled, but nodded his agreement. Ellie knew him well enough to take that as gospel.

"So you're going to get his things?" Hank asked.

"That's right."

"When will you be back?"

Snapping her head toward the door, she strutted out of the cottage and told him, "Whenever I feel like coming back."

After slamming the door behind her, Ellie kept right on strutting down the path that led away from the cottage. She couldn't have kept the grin off her face if she'd tried, and she only gathered more steam in her stride as she thought about putting her father in his place.

It was a short walk to Bernadette's Room and Board. When Ellie got there, she wanted to take another lap around town just to calm herself down. For some reason, she was no longer scared. She knew her father wasn't about to kill Clint and she knew Clint wasn't about to kill her father. That meant everyone was waiting on her for a change. That felt good.

"Good morning," Ellie chirped as she stepped into the boardinghouse.

There were two people in the front room. One was a skinny woman who sat hunched over a table and the other was a gentleman sipping from a china cup in a padded chair. Both of them looked at Ellie, but the woman was the first to speak.

"You here about a room?" she asked. Blinking a few times, she squinted and then added, "You live around here don't you?"

"Yes, ma'am," Ellie said. "I'm Hank Mason's daughter."

"Oh, the miller. I heard there was some trouble at your place last night."

Ellie looked around uncomfortably, but could only find Bernadette and the other man looking back at her. Even so, she felt nervous when she nodded and said, "Yes, there was, but it's all right now."

"Good. What do you need?"

"I'm here to collect Clint Adams's things."

"Do you know where he is?" Bernadette asked. "I've got something else he needs."

"What is it?"

"This," the skinny woman said as she motioned to the table.

Ellie only needed to see the side of the wooden frame that

was lying in front of Bernadette for her to rush over and smile gleefully. "Is that my sculpture?"

Bernadette looked down and shrugged. "It's Mr. Adams's sculpture. He hired me to fix the frame."

"What was wrong with it?" Ellie asked.

"Nothing, really. Just some chips here and there. It didn't even take as long as I thought it would to fix it. He didn't say anything about handing it over to anyone else, though."

"Well, he was bringing it to me," Ellie replied cheerfully. "I'm the one who bought it."

Bernadette's face didn't shift from the stony expression that had been on it from the start. "He didn't say anything about handing it over to anyone else."

Suddenly, all of the joy Ellie had felt in putting her foot down with her father was gone. Bernadette may not have been related to her and she may not have had a shotgun, but the skinny woman had suddenly become more immovable than Hank.

"Can I see it at least?" Ellie asked meekly.

Glancing down at the table, Bernadette shrugged. "I suppose there's no harm in that."

As Ellie crossed the room, she couldn't help but notice that the man in the chair was following her every move. Before she could get too concerned about that, Ellie reached the table and was able to see what Bernadette was working on. Actually, she barely even took notice of the frame as she pulled in a breath and covered her mouth with her hand.

"It's beautiful," Ellie sighed.

Bernadette smiled proudly and ran her fingers along the frame where she'd so recently been sanding it. "It did turn out very nice."

"When can I take it home with me? I know just where I'm going to hang it!"

"As soon as I hear from Mr. Adams. Do you know when that might be?"

"I can arrange for that later today," Ellie quickly replied.

"Good. Have him pay me a visit and I'll see that this is wrapped up and ready to go." With that, Bernadette picked up a few more tools and busied herself with one last detail on the wooden frame. It seemed that she'd already forgotten Ellie was in the room.

Ellie hurried from the boardinghouse, feeling every bit as happy as when she'd left Aunt Iris's cottage. She was so happy she didn't even realize that the man from Bernadette's sitting room had also left the boardinghouse and was rushing to catch up to her.

TWENTY-EIGHT

"Pardon me!"

Ellie rushed to the corner, ignoring whoever was shouting behind her.

"Miss! Pardon me, miss!"

Glancing quickly over her shoulder, Ellie stumbled for a few steps when she was startled by the sight of the man rushing at her. When she tried to regain her balance while also quickening her pace, Ellie only managed to make her predicament worse.

The man raced even faster to grab hold of her. Acklund got close enough to take hold of her arm before she could fall into a nearby ditch. "There you go," he said while lifting her up. "Good as new."

Flustered, Ellie patted herself while catching her breath. "I know you. You were at that boardinghouse."

Acklund smiled and nodded, having expected her to say something a lot worse. "Yes, I was. Did I hear you mention Clint Adams?"

"Yes, I did," Ellie replied with a beaming smile. "He's a good friend of mine."

"I've heard of him. He's some sort of hired gun, isn't he?"

Ellie's smile turned into a frown. "He most certainly is not. He's a good man."

"It sounds to me like you two are awfully close."

Her frown lost some of its edge, but not all of it. "We are. It seems we're going to be closer . . . if my father has his way."

Acklund grinned and chuckled. "Sounds like you have the same sort of father as I do. Tends to pull the reins in a bit too tight for a bit too long."

"He certainly does."

"Is that why you're hurrying home in such a rush?"

Ellie looked at the street ahead of her and to the cottage in the distance. Feeling foolish for having been nailed down so easily by a stranger, she shook her head. "No. I was out for a walk."

"Would you mind if I joined you?"

Knowing that her father would hate it, she curled her arm around Acklund's and nodded. "That sounds nice," she said sweetly. "My name is Ellie Mason."

"And I'm Ack . . . Ackerly." Clearing his throat to buy him some time, he winced and said, "James Ackerly."

If Ellie found his mannerisms peculiar, she was too polite to point them out. She wasn't too polite, however, to mention something else. "You're walking funny, James. Were you hurt?"

"It's my hip," Acklund replied as he raced to think of something else to tell her other than the fact that he'd recently caught a stray bullet there. Fortunately, he didn't need to do much more than look uncomfortable before Ellie took up the slack.

"I know exactly how you feel," she said. "Or I sort of know. I hurt my knee tripping over a stump when I was nine and again when I was eleven."

"Same stump?" Acklund asked.

She blushed and nodded. "It's not a very good story."

"Nonsense. Tell me all about it."

TWENTY-NINE

Acklund rode back out to his camp several hours later. Even though he knew his brother was trying to stay out of sight, he had to wonder if Mose had picked up and moved on. He caught sight of Mose's horse a few seconds before he was in danger of charging into it.

As Acklund was swinging down from his saddle, Mose hopped out from behind one of the trees that surrounded the small clearing. "Damn, Acklund, you nearly got yourself shot!"

Despite the fact that his brother was aiming a gun at him, Acklund kept his grin in place. "You can put the gun down now. Damn, you're jumpy!"

"Of course I'm jumpy," Mose replied as he squinted suspiciously at Acklund. "Last time I checked, we had a known gunman coming after us. What the hell are you so cheery about anyways?"

"I met up with someone."

"Adams? You found him when he came back to that boardinghouse?"

"No. Not him."

Mose let out a noise that sounded like a cross between spitting and steam being pushed through a piston. "I told you that was a dumb idea. Just 'cause you heard he was there once, don't mean he'd go straight back there again."

"I knew he was there," Acklund corrected. "Even heard it from the spinster that runs the place. But that ain't what's important. What's important is who I met while I was waiting."

Not only had Mose holstered his gun by now, but he'd also settled into an uncomfortable seat on the ground with one leg stretched out in front of him. "I'll bite. Who'd you meet?"

"Ellie Mason."

"Who the hell is that?"

"She's the daughter of that miller whose house Adams was holed up in."

It took a few seconds, but Mose was finally able to put the pieces together. "She didn't know who you was?"

"How would she know? I barely even got a look at her that night when all the shooting was going on. Besides, I kept to the dark and I doubt she'd remember me anyhow. I ain't some big oaf that sticks out no matter how dark it is."

Mose's long legs took up most of the ground around the remains of the campfire and his bulky frame made it difficult for Acklund to walk around him. His dirty blond hair hung over his eyes as he looked up and asked, "What's that supposed to mean?"

"Nothing."

"So you didn't find Adams?"

"No, but Ellie can send him to us. Actually, she can send him to that boardinghouse and we'll be waiting."

"Good," Mose grunted. "I'm sick of all this sneaking around. I say we just go find Dave's friends up the river and shoot the hell out of that boardinghouse as soon as Adams sticks his nose out. Then we can get back home."

"Those friends of Dave's are no good. Besides, they're probably dead already."

"I know Rob's still kickin'. He tried to get Dave to hit that stagecoach a few weeks ago, remember?"

"That's my point. They're trouble."

Mose had been poking the dead campfire with a stick,

which he now pitched angrily into the surrounding trees. "Then what the hell are we still doing here? Are we gonna kill that asshole that murdered Dave or not?"

"We will, but I don't want Ellie getting hurt. She's a nice girl."

"How nice?" Mose asked as a lewd smirk slid across his face.

"Nice enough for you to leave her the fuck alone!"

Raising his hands in surrender, Mose said, "So what makes her so damn special? Did she tell you where Adams was?"

"No, but she knows."

"And you'll make her talk?"

"I'll find out when I see her again," Acklund said. "I'm taking her out to eat."

"Huh?"

"There's a steakhouse in town and I asked her to come with me. She said yes. Can you believe it?"

Mose looked as if he'd just swallowed a horsefly. "What the fuck is wrong with you, Acklund? We ain't here so you can chase some . . ." Stopping when he saw the warning glare in his brother's eyes, Mose said, "We ain't here for this. We're here to get the asshole who killed Dave."

"Dave fell off his horse!" Acklund said. "I saw it when I was riding back into the fight. You must be blind or you would've seen it!"

"He wouldn't be dead if Adams hadn't—"

"You mean if he hadn't come up with the boneheaded idea to chase after whatever Adams was carrying. By the way, do you even know what he was carrying? It was some bunch of flowers in a frame! This whole thing is bullshit, just like every other scheme Dave tried to come up with. Momma always said he'd get himself killed one day and it looks like she was right. That don't mean we need to dig in deeper by shooting at innocent folks and maybe get our own heads blown off along the way!"

"It don't matter what Dave did," Mose said. "He may have been an idiot and he may have been a bad kid, but we could have stopped him from going on this job." Suddenly, Mose stopped himself. "Wasn't this whole thing your idea?"

"I heard about that barber sending some valuable something or other and that he hired someone to look after it. Dave's the one who decided to go after it with guns blazing."

A shadow came over Mose's face, but he couldn't get himself to dispute the claim. "He was still our brother."

"And I'm the one that buried him. I'm always the one to clean up his mess. It seems like something good might come out of this bullshit, so I'm not gonna let it pass me by."

Throwing up his hands, Mose said, "All right, but if you're gonna piss around with some woman, then I'm going to go round up Dave's friends. Maybe they give a damn that his killer is still roaming around, free as a bird."

"Those boys will just get angry and drunk like they always do. You really think they'll decide to come and help out of the goodness of their hearts?"

"I aim to find out. Are you comin' with me or not?"

Acklund stood his ground mostly because he'd never liked being pushed around by his older brother. He also knew that most everything he wanted to say would just make things worse. "I'm staying. Someone needs to. Otherwise, Adams will be able to ride off whenever he likes without anyone being the wiser."

"Yeah. You're right, I guess."

When Mose got up and stormed to where his horse was tied, Acklund wanted to stop him. Unfortunately, he recognized the look in Mose's eyes all too well. Mose wouldn't be stopped without a fight and Acklund still felt too good to fight. Besides, a little more help wouldn't hurt and it would take some time for him to get it.

THIRTY

"This is a bad idea, you know," Clint said.

Hank hadn't come to check in on him since Ellie had left, but he knew the old man was still in the cottage. He could hear every creak and every knock coming from the other room, and Clint was certain Hank was still well within the sound of his voice.

"The law is bound to check in on me sooner or later," Clint added. "Folks will realize I'm missing and it's well known I was last seen with you and your daughter."

While that may have been stretching the truth just a bit, Clint knew that Bernadette wouldn't hold onto the flower picture forever. She also wouldn't tolerate him leaving his things in his room without paying for it. There was always the possibility of her storing his saddlebags in a closet, but Clint wasn't about to mention that.

"So you really think I won't tell anyone about this?" Clint asked. "I've got to get my hands free sometime. What kind of a husband would I be if I was always tied up?"

Clint had been keeping that up ever since Ellie had stepped out the door. He wasn't sure exactly how long ago that was, but even he could tell his constant chattering was taking its toll. By the time Hank finally got up from where he'd been sitting and stomped into the bedroom, Clint was sick of hearing his own voice.

"I already told you the preacher is a friend of mine!" Hank growled. "And don't worry about the law neither. Deputy Cale is useful as tits on a bull, but he'll trust me over you any day."

"What about my hands?" Clint asked.

"What about 'em?"

"Will the ropes be coming off or will I spend my married life tied to this bed?"

Hank scowled and replied, "If I had my way . . ."

"I figured as much. What about Ellie? She's a grown woman. She can make her own decisions where a husband is concerned."

"If she could do that, she would'a done it already. She's a pretty girl, but she don't know how to land a man. I figure a man like you is better than the sort that'll try to get her just to . . . get her."

"I'm flattered. It sounds like you think awfully highly of me."

"I haven't knocked you in the head again, have I? After all the gum flappin' you've been doing, I'd say that's damn close to saintly."

"You know what would push you the rest of the way to sainthood?" Clint asked. "Get me out of these ropes so I can stretch my legs."

"Not yet."

"How about loosening them?"

Hank shook his head.

Clint sighed and leaned his head against the bedpost. "Can I at least have some water and maybe something to eat? My head's killing me from where you knocked me out."

Glaring down at Clint with a face that was an unreadable mask, Hank let out a slow, measured breath. Just when it seemed the old man was about to shake his head and grouse some more, he nodded. "I can get you some water. Maybe a little grub to go with it."

"Mighty neighborly of you," Clint said.

Hank obviously didn't know what to make of the friendly tone in Clint's voice. He turned away from the bed, took a few steps toward the door, and then rushed back to get a look at Clint. When he saw that Clint hadn't moved a muscle, he grumbled to himself and left the room for good.

Clint kept his head back and his eyes closed. That way, he wasn't distracted by the sight of the wall or hints of sunlight coming through the square window. It was easier to concentrate on the sounds drifting through the room. What he was most interested in were Hank's steps and eventually the subtle squeak as the old man carefully opened the door. Keeping his eyes closed, Clint thought back to the last time he'd been outside the cottage. It took a few moments, but he remembered there had been a water pump just outside and to the right of the cottage's front door. Since that was on the opposite corner of the bedroom, Clint allowed himself to make a bit of noise as he stretched and scraped to get his hands loose.

The ropes were fairly well tied, but Clint had been pulling at the knots from the moment he'd regained consciousness. His wrists burned and his ankles felt as if they'd been snapped within his boots, but he'd managed to give himself a little more slack than when he'd started. Taking advantage of the time when Hank was outside, Clint shifted his weight until he could curl his legs closer to his hands.

Unfortunately, he still wasn't close enough to get to the knife in his boot. He knew the slender blade was still in its spot because he could feel it against his ankle. Knowing it was there may have been comforting, but getting the knife in his hand was going to make him feel a whole lot better. Mostly, Clint was grateful that Hank was such a piss-poor jailer.

Wincing at the noise he was making, Clint knocked the side of his boot against the floor a few times. He did his best to time it to the screeching coming from the rusty pump handle outside, but still expected to hear Hank rush back into the cottage at any second. When the old man didn't hurry back, Clint kept working the knife out of its scabbard.

After shaking his leg a few times, Clint felt more like a dog wagging its tail. As ridiculous as it may have looked, he was getting the job done. The slender boot knife was slipping free, thanks to the fact that he kept it loose in its scabbard anyway so he could get to it in a pinch.

The squeaking from the pump handle stopped.

Hank's heavy steps pounded against the porch and would carry him into the cottage at any second.

Clint gave his feet one last knock, which was enough to drop the knife from his boot. He pulled a few muscles along the way, but Clint was just able to straighten his legs out again and use them to cover the knife on the floor before Hank walked in.

"Here's some water," Hank said as he held a dented ladle to Clint's mouth.

Most of the water spilled down the front of Clint's shirt, but some of it managed to get down his throat. Clint was grateful for the water, but he was more concerned with Hank catching sight of the blade or knife handle protruding from under Clint's legs.

"You want more?"

As much as he wanted another drink, Clint shook his head. "No, that'll do."

"How about I fix you some eggs? It's all we got."

"That'd be good."

Hank studied Clint for a few seconds before grunting and turning his back to him. The old man's footsteps stopped a bit short, so Clint resisted the urge to move his legs.

After a few more seconds, Hank grunted again and stepped out of the doorway. Whatever the old man had been hoping to see, he hadn't seen enough to keep spying.

The moment Clint heard pans rattling from the other room, he stretched his arms to loosen the ropes tying him to the bedpost and scooted the knife closer.

THIRTY-ONE

The square window overhead was dimming as the day wore into night, but Clint wasn't paying much attention to it. Hank grumbled to himself as he stomped about the cottage, but the old man seemed more concerned with his daughter than his prisoner. In fact, after throwing some eggs in the general direction of Clint's mouth, Hank had spent the better part of the day muttering at the front window.

Clint lost track of his knife after kicking it a bit too hard one time, but he'd loosed his ropes enough to get hold of it once he knew where it had landed. After that, he'd whiled away the hours getting the knife in hand and positioning it so he could rake the blade against his ropes. The next snag Clint had hit was the discovery that Hank Mason was smart enough to use quality rope.

The thick lengths that had cut into Clint's wrists weren't snapping as quickly as Clint had hoped once he'd put the knife to use. In fact, Clint started to wonder if the blade was having any impact at all. Just to be certain it was, Clint tried to tug the knife side to side instead of back and forth. The blade hardly moved, which told him it was within a groove of some sort. It wasn't much, but it was better than if he'd realized the blade hadn't even cut through the bindings. Gritting his teeth, Clint got back to work.

As soon as he started in again, Clint heard Hank's familiar stomping steps rushing toward the bedroom. Clint hadn't realized the old man could move so fast, and it was all he could do to try to close his hands around the knife before it was discovered.

When Hank came into the bedroom, he was carrying his shotgun. The moment he was close enough, Hank stuck both barrels under Clint's chin and snarled, "Where is she?"

"I haven't left this spot," Clint protested.

"Don't give me any bullshit! Ellie's been gone all goddamn day, now where did she go?"

"I . . . don't . . . know."

It seemed clear that Hank wasn't satisfied with that response. Clint strained against the ropes to try to snap them because the old man looked mad enough to pull his trigger no matter what came out of Clint's mouth.

Suddenly, the squeak of the front door's hinges caused Hank's ears to prick up. Turning quickly enough to crack the shotgun's barrel against Clint's jaw, he stormed into the next room.

Clint had to get out of there and he had to do it now. The only reason he'd been so easy on Hank was because he could understand why the old man had gotten himself so worked up. He also figured that Hank knew he was in too deep to just let Clint go. Either that, or Hank was just too stubborn to do so. Either way, Clint was convinced he'd be safe until he got himself out.

All of that changed when Clint saw the angry fire in Hank's eyes. Judging by the voices coming from the next room, that fire wasn't about to die down anytime soon.

"Where the hell were you, little girl?" Hank roared.

Despite the rage in her father's voice, Ellie's remained chipper. "I went to buy a new dress."

"All this time to get a dress?"

"And I went to Clint's boardinghouse. I saw my flowers and they were so pretty!"

After a sputtering pause, Hank asked, "What in the blazes is wrong with you? Are you touched in the head?"

"Of course not. Is Clint still here?"

"Of course he's here. Where can he go?"

"He's still tied up?" Ellie cried. "You said you'd let him go! You promised!"

"After Mike got back to—"

"Oh, for heaven's sake!" With that, Ellie's lighter footsteps fluttered toward the bedroom.

Clint didn't bother hiding the knife, since his renewed efforts had dug the blade in twice as deep as it had been before. He looked toward the door and did his best to keep her looking at his face instead of his hands. "Have you talked any sense into your father?" he asked.

"Pa's real upset," she whispered. "But I have good news."

"What?"

"I met a man and I think he's . . . I think . . . I know I felt something the moment I saw him. He felt it, too, and I'm meeting him for—"

"What?" Clint bellowed in a voice that boomed almost as much as Hank's. "Just get me . . ." Dropping his voice to a harsh whisper, Clint said, "At least get that shotgun away from your father. After that, I don't care what you do or who you meet."

"I don't know if I can."

"Do you want to be married to me?" Clint asked.

She winced and lowered her eyes. "I don't want to hurt you, but—"

"Neither do I," Clint snapped so he could finish her meandering thought. "Give me a chance to get out of here and we can both be on our separate ways. I also suggest you get the hell away from that crazy father of yours."

Seeing the confused look in Ellie's eyes, Clint had to wonder if Hank hadn't been right about one thing at least. Her being touched in the head, even just a little, would go a long way to explain a lot of things. Finally, she collected herself and straightened up. There wasn't as much confusion in her eyes, but Clint wasn't about to take comfort from that just yet.

"I'm leaving," she declared.

Clint's jaw dropped as Hank walked into the room. Both

of them tried to put some words together, but Ellie cut them off.

"I need some time to figure something out," Ellie said. "Pa, I want you to let Clint go. If he runs away from me now, he'll only run away once we're married."

"No, he . . . I mean . . ." But Hank wasn't able to refute his daughter's point. In fact, it seemed all the holes in his hasty plan of action were now showing through like a fishing net that unraveled after a pivotal strand had been cut.

"Fine," she snapped. "I'll do it myself. If you want to stop me, then you'll just have to shoot me." With that, Ellie knelt down beside Clint and reached for the knot that was positioned on the back side of his wrists.

Before she could get close enough to see the knife he'd been hiding, Clint set it down and pushed it under the bed. To cover the sounds, he shifted his weight and made sure to kick his heels against the floor plenty of times in the process. As a way to explain his sudden squirming fit as well as provide a bit more noise, Clint asked, "What's going on here? He's just going to shoot me the first chance he gets!"

"No, he won't," Ellie replied. "I'll guarantee it. Won't I, Pa?"

Hank was too flustered to speak, but he wasn't about to shoot his own daughter. Rather than agree or disagree with Ellie, he stormed away.

"You trust me, don't you Clint?" she asked as she pulled at the knot.

Now that he didn't need to cover any strange noises, Clint nodded and quietly replied, "Sure. Just think about what you're doing."

"I am thinking. That's why I need some time."

Ellie got the ropes loose and had done the same for Clint's ankles by the time he'd shaken free of the ropes around his wrists. When he managed to get to his feet, Ellie was already gone.

THIRTY-TWO

Within seconds after he stood up, Clint nearly fell back down again. After sitting for so long in the same position, the only thing he could feel in his legs was a throbbing pain. With the ropes having been so tight around his ankles, his feet were nothing but deadweight inside his boots. Steadying himself on the bed with one hand, Clint wheeled around to face the heavy steps that came at him like a one-man stampede from the next room.

"This is your fault, goddammit!" Carrying the shotgun in front of him, Hank roared as he flew at Clint.

Clint reacted out of instinct and reached for the shotgun with both hands. He started to lose his balance again, but not until after he'd grabbed the double-barreled weapon and shoved it toward the wall. When he fell onto the bed, Clint maintained his grip and let his momentum rip the shotgun completely from Hank's grip. When he rolled to the other side of the mattress, Clint prayed his legs would support him.

"What are you gonna do now?" Hank snarled, "You gonna shoot me? Go on and shoot me!"

Having gone from squirming on the floor to jumping up and fighting to pull away the shotgun, Clint's breathing was hard and ragged. The feeling was coming back to his feet and legs, but they still felt as if they were being worked over by scores of cold needles.

"I don't want to shoot you!" Clint said. "All I want is—"

Before Clint could finish his sentence, Hank lowered his shoulder and charged. "Fine, then," the old man grunted. "Your mistake."

Clint didn't think to pull the shotgun's triggers, even though that would have been a real quick end to a real bad day. He didn't even get a chance to rethink his position when Hank slammed into him and took Clint off his feet.

Both men rolled onto the bed and fell off the other side in a heap. Clint hit the floor on his shoulder and swore under his breath as his arm jammed awkwardly into his body. Fortunately, it wasn't the arm that had so recently been stitched.

Hank wrapped his hands around the shotgun and tried to reclaim the weapon for himself. While he was able to pull the shotgun closer, he couldn't break Clint's hold on it. He gritted his teeth, leaned back, and pounded his knee against Clint's ribs.

The blow emptied Clint's lungs, but also spurred him on. He crumpled to play up how much it hurt, waited for Hank to move in for another shot, and then snapped his right shoulder toward the old man's chin. It was a glancing blow at best, but it shocked Hank enough to give Clint some room to move. Both of them struggled to get back to their feet, which meant they inadvertently helped the other one up.

All four hands were locked around the shotgun. Hank pulled the gun toward his chest and Clint tugged in the opposite direction. Pouring in just a little bit more strength, Clint waited to feel Hank's response. Just as Clint had hoped, Hank doubled his own effort to get the shotgun away from him.

Suddenly, Clint reversed his own direction so he was pushing as Hank pulled. That way, all of the momentum was aimed at Hank and all Clint had to do was twist to give that momentum a nudge in the right direction.

The butt of the shotgun cracked against Hank's face and sent the man reeling. Blood sprayed from a cut in his chin, which Hank wiped away using his shirtsleeve. The ferocity in his eyes dimmed somewhat when he saw Clint open the breech of the shotgun to drop both shells onto the floor.

"There," Clint said as he tossed the weapon to the other side of the room. "Is this finished now?"

"You'd like that, wouldn't you?"

"Yes!" Clint exclaimed. "I would! All I ever wanted to do was deliver a goddamn painting!"

"But you . . . you and Ellie . . ."

"That was between me and her," Clint said. "She's not a little girl any more. Get used to the idea."

"I'm just trying to do the right thing."

"Really? You think knocking me out, tying me up, and trying to force me to marry your daughter is the right thing? I'd hate to see what you think is the wrong thing." Watching the old man sputter, Clint let out a breath and asked, "Where's my gun?"

"So you are gonna—"

"I'm gonna take my property back. Then I'm gonna deliver that damn painting or whatever the hell it is and I'm gonna get the hell away from this place. You got any objections to that?"

Slowly, Hank shook his head.

"Now where's my gun?"

THIRTY-THREE

Acklund arrived at the little restaurant, expecting to be plenty early for his supper with Ellie. After dealing with his brother and watching Mose storm away like a kid with his nose bent out of joint, Acklund hoped he wasn't too cross to enjoy anyone's company. He realized the error in that thinking the moment he saw Ellie sitting at one of the front tables, wrapped up in a new dress with green ribbons.

"You look pretty," Acklund said. "How long have you been here?"

"Not long," Ellie snapped as she practically jumped to her feet.

The sudden move made Acklund jump as well. He twitched and started thinking of what he would tell her when she asked him about his part in shooting up her father's house. He was caught even more off his guard when Ellie smiled warmly and approached him.

"It's good to see you," she said. "Really good."

"What's wrong?"

"Things are just all tangled up. There's a man. His name is Clint and at first I thought he was so handsome and so heroic. He stepped in and helped me and my father. Now I wish I hadn't seen him."

Acklund scowled fiercely when he asked, "Did he hurt you?"

"No. It's just that . . . my father wants me to do something and Clint wants me to do something else and I'm just sick of hearing it. I tried to put a stop to it, but I don't know what I can do or even if there is something I can do about it."

"What do you want?"

She blinked and shrugged. "Right now, I want to be where nobody else can find me and pull me back into that mess."

"I know just how you feel. Would you like to meet some other time?"

Ellie smiled. "When I said nobody else, that didn't include you. I'm glad you found me."

"Well, I'm hungry. Do you still want to get something to eat?"

"Yes. A friend of mine cooks at a hotel on First Street. She could make us something. It wouldn't be much."

"That sounds good." Offering her his arm, Acklund put on his best smile and asked, "Shall we?"

"Yes," Ellie replied. "I think we shall."

Acklund hadn't been expecting this. He hadn't been expecting to find someone like Ellie or to have her actually want to be with him for more than a few seconds. He hadn't expected Dave to get killed or for Mose to seek out Dave's outlaw friends instead of listening to his own flesh and blood. Rather than go against it and keep counting up the things he hadn't been expecting, Acklund decided to have supper with Ellie and enjoy the things that *had* gone his way.

Dave may have been a rambunctious, pigheaded fool, but he had taught Acklund something: Life was short and it could end at any second.

Acklund allowed himself to be led to a small kitchen that serviced a little hotel. Ellie's friend cooked up steaks that had been set aside on account of all the gristle hanging from them, as well as some mashed potatoes that were left over from dinner service for the guests. It was the best meal Acklund had had in a good, long while.

THIRTY-FOUR

Clint's gun belt was buckled securely around his waist as he walked out of Aunt Iris's cottage. Just to be certain, he opened the cylinder and checked to see if the gun was loaded. Hank wasn't a complete idiot, which meant the gun was empty but there were still plenty of rounds in the loops of his belt. Clint stuffed fresh bullets into the Colt, snapped the cylinder shut, and glanced over his shoulder.

Since he'd gotten his gun back, Clint had been waiting for the old man to make another move. He didn't turn his back on Hank until the door was shut between them. Even then, Clint was ready to be shot in the back. After he'd put some space between himself and the cottage, Clint realized the old man had played his hand as far as it could go.

Hank didn't take a shot at him. He didn't even watch Clint through the cottage's windows. Even so, Clint didn't feel safe until he'd rounded a corner without incident. His first stop was the stable. If he'd taken someone as prisoner, one of the first things he would do would be to get the man's horse. Apparently, Hank hadn't planned for that either. Eclipse was right where Clint had left him when he'd first decided to stay in town for more than a few hours. After looking the Darley Arabian over and patting his neck for good measure, Clint left the stable.

"You gonna be stayin' around for another day or two?" the stableman asked.

Without turning around, Clint replied, "Not if I can help it."

"You owe me for anything after tonight."

"I'm good for it." Since he'd already built up a head of steam, Clint intended on leaving it at that. If the stableman wanted an advance payment that badly, he would just have to come and get it for himself.

Apparently, the other man wasn't so anxious to stake that claim.

Clint's next stop was Bernadette's Room and Board. He pushed open the door hard enough to make it slam against the wall. Even though he hadn't expected to make so much noise, he was surprised at how little of a reaction his entrance created.

Bernadette looked up from her desk and asked, "Where have you been?"

"It's a long story," Clint replied.

"Well, don't think that means you're getting out of paying for your room. It was reserved on your account, which means I couldn't rent it out to anyone else."

As far as Clint could tell, there wasn't anyone else in the place, but he wasn't about to argue the point.

"Speaking of your account," Bernadette continued, "that picture of yours is done."

"Picture? Oh, that."

"Didn't your little friend tell you?"

Clint narrowed his eyes and growled, "What little friend?"

"The girl with the brown hair. She said she knew you. I think her name was Nellie." Shrugging, she added, "Seemed sweet enough, but a little scatterbrained."

"That'd be Ellie."

"So you do know her."

"Yes," Clint groaned. "She was here?"

Bernadette nodded as she got up from her desk. She closed the ledger in which she'd been writing and then walked over to the table that took up most of the dining room. "She said she wanted to pick up your things. I guess she forgot about that when she got a look at this picture of yours. She wanted to take that with her as well, but I wouldn't let her until I heard from you. She got all worked up and left in a huff. I think she forgot about picking up your things."

Rubbing his face as if he simply didn't know what to do with his hands, Clint asked, "Is the frame repaired?"

"Good as new," Bernadette said proudly.

Grabbing the frame with enough force to make Bernadette cringe, Clint looked it over from all sides. It hadn't been long since he'd seen it, but by this time he was just sick of the damn thing. "How much do I owe you?" he asked.

"I have it all figured up here," she replied as she handed over a small piece of folded paper. "It's your bill. If you intend on staying longer—"

"I don't. How much extra to deliver this to Hank Mason's house?"

"Fifty cents?" Bernadette replied hesitantly.

Without a blink, Clint said, "Fine. Tack it onto the bill and deliver it as soon as you get the chance. Here's your money."

Judging by the look on Bernadette's face, she was upset that she hadn't pushed her delivery fee a little higher. She took the money and said, "Wait here and I'll get your change."

"Keep it. Thanks for all you've done."

It took Bernadette a moment to hear through Clint's gruff tone and digest his intent. When she did, she smiled and replied, "You're welcome. Anytime you're back in town, be sure to come on over. Will you be riding out of here soon?"

"That's the idea."

"Then wait right here." Clint started to protest, but Bernadette waved it off. "I made some food for you, but you never ate it. The least I can do is wrap it up so you can take it with you."

While Bernadette was in the kitchen, Clint had a few moments to think. The first thing that came to mind was something else the thin brunette had mentioned before. He walked to the kitchen and found her bundling something up in a rag. "You said that Ellie was worked up about something?"

"That's right."

"What was it?"

"The flowers. She said she was going to get you to pick them up early, but she never came back."

"And she never mentioned it to me," Clint said. "Was there anything else that distracted her?"

Bernadette finished tying up the rag, but got a guilty look on her face. "Actually, there was another fellow here who was waiting for you. As soon as that scatterbrained girl left, he went after her."

"What man?"

"I never got his name or what he wanted. He didn't even leave a note."

"Why didn't you tell me about that?" Clint asked.

"Because," Bernadette said sternly, "he didn't leave a name or note. What was there to tell? I did glance out the window after they left and the two of them met up outside. They walked away together and seemed awful close."

Clint guessed that little bit of spying was behind the guilty look on Bernadette's face. "Do you recall what he looked like?"

"About your height. Longer hair, rougher face."

The more Bernadette said, the clearer the picture in Clint's mind became. It was a picture of Mose's brother, Acklund. "Did he carry a gun?"

"Yes."

"Was anyone else with him? A taller fellow with light hair?"

Bernadette didn't have to think about that one. "No. He walked with a limp, though. Favored his left side. You know him?"

"I think so," Clint replied as he accepted the bundle of food from her. "I just hope I'm wrong."

THIRTY-FIVE

Clint approached Aunt Iris's cottage the way he might approach a hornet's nest. Every step was tentative and every one of the hairs on his arms stood up as if the possibility of being stung was a current that ran through the air. His eyes were fixed upon the quiet little building and his hand never strayed from the holster at his side.

He was surprised to get all the way to the front door without seeing Hank or at least the barrel of his shotgun poking from one of the windows. When he knocked, Clint didn't hear so much as a rustle from the other side of the door.

Since nobody seemed to be at home, Clint went to the Mason house. He approached that place even more carefully. The house was surrounded with more homes and a few other people walking between them, so there were plenty of sounds to catch Clint's ear. He went up and knocked on the door a bit quicker this time, but got the same result he'd gotten at the cottage.

"You lookin' for Hank or Ellie?"

Turning toward the sound of that voice, Clint found an old woman sitting in a rocker on the porch of the neighboring house. "Hank," he replied. "You seen him?"

"Nope. He must be at the mill."

"What about Ellie?"

The old woman's face already looked like a prune that had been soaked in river water and left out to shrivel in the sun. The wrinkles became even deeper as she scrunched her face in concentration. Finally, she told him, "Nope. Ain't seen her either. You know where they been?"

"No," Clint said as he wondered why he'd even hoped for something to go smoothly in this town. "I haven't seen them."

As Clint walked away, the old lady kept right on talking. She had speculations on the weather and gossip about the rest of the neighbors, but Clint didn't pay any attention to her. He was grateful as soon as he was far enough from the house that he couldn't hear her voice. As he approached Knee Bend Creek, the rushing water and the creaking wood of the mill's wheel filled his ears.

Pete was doing something at the edge of the creek and he stood up the moment he got a look at Clint. "Hey Hank!" he shouted. "That man from the other day is back!"

A few seconds later, Hank shoved open the door to the mill and came outside. "There were plenty of men about over the last few days, you simpleminded fool! Which one was . . ." The moment he caught sight of Clint, Hank stopped in his tracks and fell silent.

"See?" Pete grunted. "Now he's the man from today."

"Shut your mouth and fix the wheel like I asked," Hank said.

Pete got to his feet and ran to the wheel.

"What the hell do you want?" the old man asked.

"Where's Ellie?" Clint asked. Before he could give a word of explanation, he saw a fire light in Hank's eyes. "She might be in danger. Have you seen her?"

"The only danger she's in is because of you. Now get the hell off my property before I have you tossed out on yer ear!"

"You're right," Clint said, which clearly threw Hank for a loop. "It might be partly my fault, because one of those men that came after me might have gotten ahold of her."

Hank stormed away from the door and charged at Clint. Considering the old man's shotgun or any other weapon had to be inside the mill, Clint was glad to have drawn him onto neutral ground. "What are you sayin' to me, boy?" Hank snarled.

"I'm not certain, but one of those men might have decided to go after Ellie. I could be wrong, but I thought I'd check in to find her for myself. If you know where she is, you can just tell me and I'll be on my way. I didn't come to make any trouble."

Narrowing his squint even more, Hank asked, "You didn't? So Ellie is really in trouble?"

"Do you know where she is? You don't have to tell me where she is," Clint added. "Do you at least know?"

"No," Hank admitted. "I don't."

"Then she might be in trouble."

THIRTY-SIX

It had only been a matter of hours, but Ellie and Acklund spoke to each other as if they were lifelong friends. They didn't even touch upon any pressing matters or important topics. All they did was swap stories along with a few jokes to make the night fly past in a rush.

When the restaurant was closing its doors, Ellie had pleaded with her friend to let them stay. After the cook had left and the cleaning was done, her friend was anxious to leave and practically shoved both of them through the door. "If you want to stay any longer," the friend had told them, "you'll have to rent a room."

Ellie stood outside the hotel and looked at the locked door to the restaurant on the lower floor. "Well," she sighed, "I guess I should go."

"Your father's probably worried sick, huh?" Acklund asked.

"Yes. Probably."

"Maybe you should . . ." At that moment, Acklund heard the rumble of horses galloping down the street. He looked in that direction and saw a group of three men rounding the corner and heading straight for the hotel. The riders didn't pull back on their reins, allowing the horses to tear through town like a storm.

Night had fallen some time ago, leaving only a few torches scattered along the side of the street to give off any light. Even in the darkness, Acklund could pick out Mose's blond hair fluttering like a dirty flag from the big man's head. Before his brother or the other two riders could get a good look at him, Acklund grabbed Ellie so he stood between her and Mose.

"Maybe we should do what your friend suggested," Acklund said.

Ellie laughed nervously and shook her head. "I don't think that would be such a good—"

Acklund cut her off by pressing his lips against hers. He also pulled her closer so her face was hidden as Mose and the other two men rode past. Even after the rumble of nearby hooves faded away, Acklund kept kissing her.

The longer their lips remained together, the more heat they could feel from one another. Acklund lost sight of any other reason he'd had in starting the kiss and Ellie wasn't at all eager to finish it. In fact, she pressed in tight against him and opened her mouth a bit so she could run the tip of her tongue along Acklund's mouth.

By the time Mose and the others had rounded a corner and gone out of sight, Acklund was reluctant to break away from her. Somehow, he forced himself to do so.

"Could you do me a favor?" he asked.

Ellie replied in a breathless sigh. "What?"

"Could you stay here? Just wait for me inside. There's something I need to do and I don't want you to go home just yet."

When she moved her head, it was difficult for Acklund to tell whether Ellie was nodding or just leaning back for some air. "I won't go anywhere," she said.

"Good." Before Acklund could take two steps toward the street, he was stopped by a powerful grip around his arm.

Ellie grabbed hold of him as if she were about to pull his arm from its socket. "Where are you going?" she asked urgently.

"There's something I need to take care of."

"Can't it wait?"

The hunger in Ellie's eyes was unmistakable. Her grip on him held a world of promise and even the tone in her voice got a fire burning deep inside of Acklund's body. Even with all of that, he somehow got himself to say, "No. It can't wait."

"Hurry back, then."

"You've got my word on that."

But Ellie wasn't about to let him go just yet. When he'd moved to the end of her reach only to be pulled back again, Acklund found her staring at him intently.

"When I said hurry, I meant it," she told him. "I don't want this night to be done, but I won't wait forever."

"Don't worry. You won't be waiting long."

Apparently, that was what she wanted to hear. Ellie renewed the smile on her face and let go of Acklund's arm. She stayed in front of the hotel until he'd rounded the corner and left her sight.

From there, Acklund broke into a run and didn't stop until he got to the spot where he'd tied his horse.

THIRTY-SEVEN

Acklund moved as if his tail were on fire. He ran to his horse so quickly that its four legs beneath him hardly got him moving faster than the two of his own. He snapped his reins and didn't let up until he'd caught sight of Mose and the two riders accompanying him. He came up on the three men so fast that they all drew their guns and turned on him before they made it back to the brothers' camp.

"Acklund?" Mose shouted as he squinted into the shadows. "That you?"

"Hell, yes, it's me!"

"You gotta stop runnin' up on me like that. I'm liable to—"

"Who are these men?" Acklund asked before Mose could finish his threat.

The big blond man sat tall in his saddle and nodded at each rider flanking him. "These are Dave's friends," he said with a proud grin. "That's Al and that's Rob."

The two riders seemed to be about Dave's age, which made Acklund look at them as if they were kids. Even though Dave had only been a few years Acklund's junior, Dave had always been the little brother. Therefore, "little" came to mind when Acklund looked at the men who'd been Dave's friends.

Al kept his beady eyes fixed upon Acklund and gave him a short wave when Acklund looked back at him. Al had long hair the color of trampled straw, which was tied behind his head like a horse's tail. His buckskin jacket had seen many nights in the wilderness, and the bone-handled knife strapped across his belly was well-worn with daily use.

Although just as rough around the edges, Rob looked like he'd been spawned from wild animals instead of just hunting them. His dark hair sprung from his scalp at odd angles to form a bush on top of his head. A thick goatee may not have covered his entire face, but it kept most of his mouth from being seen. As a greeting, he gave Acklund a lazy upward nod, which also caused his chin to sag as if that part of him was tied to his chest. Now that he moved a bit, it became obvious that his eyes didn't exactly focus on the same spot.

"So you boys knew our brother?" Acklund asked.

"That's right," Rob said with a distinctive drawl. "An' he told us plenty about you two."

It was obvious Rob wanted to be asked what had been discussed, but Acklund ignored him and shifted his eyes to Al. "What did you and Dave do?"

"We robbed the Union Pacific line a few years back," Al said.

"The whole line, huh?"

"No. Just the—"

"So you're outlaws," Acklund said impatiently. "Why should you get involved with family business?"

"Hey!" Rob snapped. "Mose asked us to come along. Dave was our friend and we don't want the asshole who killed him to walk away pretty as you please."

"Then you're out to kill a horse," Acklund said. "Because that's how Dave died. He fell off a horse. You still want blood?"

Al glanced at Mose, but Rob kept his crooked eyes pointed in Acklund's general direction and didn't bother to close his mouth as he exhaled like a bass.

"We was told there was another gunman who killed him," Al said. "A man by the name of Adams."

"That's right, but—"

"Ain't no buts about it, Acklund," Mose roared. "Adams was there and it's because of him Dave's dead. If you don't give a shit, then leave the job to us who do."

"What job?" Acklund demanded. "The job that got us into this mess was Dave's stupid idea."

"You came along this far," Mose pointed out. "You shot up that house with them folks in it just to put down the mangy dog that killed Dave. You remember that?"

"Sure I do. Somewhere while we were getting shot at, I realized we were on a fool's errand. Dave's still dead and Adams was defending himself just like any one of us would've done."

Scowling with confused anger, Mose said, "You went into town to find Adams! You told me you found where he was stayin' and that you could figure out where we could hit him again so we could finish the bastard."

"I know. Maybe it took a while for me to see things differently, but they're plenty clear now. When I was sittin' there I—"

"Wait," Mose growled. "You didn't go there to find Adams so we could kill him. You probably went there to warn him!"

Reaching for his knife, Al snarled, "No good traitor!"

Acklund drew his .38 and pointed it at Al before the other man could get his blade clear of its scabbard. "Keep your nose out of this, goddammit! This is between me and my brother."

"Dave was like a brother to us," Rob said as he used one eye to sight along the top of his own pistol. He was close enough to make his aim accurate enough to hit someone.

Mose skinned his gun and immediately pointed it at Rob. "Don't forget yer place, boy," he said in a tone that he'd used on all his little brothers at one time or another.

Letting out a grunting sigh, Rob lowered his gun.

"We've had our time to simmer down, Mose," Acklund said. "Haven't you had time to think about what we're doing? Doesn't it seem like we could be in too deep? I've heard of Clint Adams. He could kill us easy, but he didn't even do that when we were ambushing him. He could've gunned Dave down without a thought, but he didn't. Maybe this was all a mistake."

"Mistake, my ass," Mose shot back. "If you're afraid of Adams, then just ride on home."

Acklund lowered his pistol and dropped it into its holster. He knew his older brother well enough to recognize when a notion was wedged so deeply into his head that nobody could pull it out. Dave being killed had only wedged it in that much deeper. He looked around at the other two men, but knew better than to think they'd talk any sense.

As if to prove Acklund right, Rob said, "I ain't afraid of no man. The four of us can kill Clint Adams."

"We'll do it right there in town," Al added. "Middle of the afternoon, so everyone can see."

"So everyone can see?" Acklund chuckled. "Jesus, you really are just as stupid as Dave was."

"What the hell happened to you, brother?" Mose asked. "Don't you know blood is thicker than anything?"

"I know that. I just came to my senses is all. Hopefully, you'll do the same before you let these two idiots turn you into a wanted man or, worse yet, a dead one."

"You set out with the two of us to rob that fella," Mose pointed out.

"And it was a mistake. So is this." Tired of talking to a bunch of fools who didn't want to listen, Acklund turned his back to them and rode away.

THIRTY-EIGHT

It was getting late and Clint still hadn't caught sight of Ellie. Hinterland wasn't a big town, so it didn't take Clint long to ride up and down every street, circle back, and ride them again. He checked in at Aunt Iris's cottage, but it was just as quiet and dark as the Mason house. Somewhere along the line, it seemed Clint had lost track of Hank as well.

Clint rode back to the mill, but it was closed up.

He looked in on Bernadette, but the slender woman hadn't even left her spot. She swore to tell Clint if she saw Ellie when she delivered the picture, but he was afraid that would be too late. If those gunmen had Ellie, Clint couldn't afford to waste a single moment. For all he knew, she could already be dead.

Dead or worse.

Rather than retrace his steps a third time, Clint decided to stop and think. There were enough thoughts rattling in his head to fill his ears with a jangling sound, so he decided to do something about that, too.

Normally, Clint wouldn't have chosen a place like the Howling Moon Saloon to sit and gather his thoughts. While the rest of town was settling in for the night, the Howling Moon was living up to its name. Card games were getting rowdy, the piano player was banging on the keys as if they'd wronged him, and the drunks were getting boisterous. Compared to the aggravation that had filled the last few of his days, sitting in the middle of that storm did Clint a lot of good. At least he knew what to expect.

"Hey, there!" the bartender said as he walked over to where Clint was standing. "If it isn't the great Clint Adams."

"Not so great, but Clint Adams all the same," Clint corrected.

"Fair enough. What can I get for you?"

"How about a beer?"

"Sure thing!"

Noticing that the barkeep seemed to be gearing up for an announcement, Clint leaned forward and said, "A beer and nothing else to go along with it."

"Ben told me not to let you pay for your own drinks while you're here," the barkeep said. "He also made it clear that you should be known as a hero in this place."

"I'll pay for my own beer, just as long as I can drink it in some peace and quiet."

Patting the top of the bar, the barkeep nodded. "Just trying to liven up the place. Most men like a bit of fanfare."

"Your place seems lively enough already. I'll just take a beer."

The barkeep filled a glass to the brim and set it down in front of Clint. When he saw the money in Clint's hand, he said, "Still on the house, friend."

"Much obliged. Say, would you happen to recall if there was anyone else that came in here? Maybe someone during that little party Ben threw for me?"

After thinking it over for a second, the barkeep winced. "A whole lot of men were in here. Soon as someone starts buying drinks, they flock to my bar like vultures."

"That's what I figured," Clint replied with a shrug. After that, he took a drink of his beer and savored the bitter taste of it.

"What did the fellas look like?"

Glancing up as if he were surprised the barkeep was still standing there, Clint told him, "One was a big man with blond hair and a dumb face. The other was about my height with stringy hair. Both of them would have been armed."

"The smaller one have a limp?"

Holding his glass up without drinking from it, Clint said, "Yeah. He was shot in his right hip."

"That's the one. I saw him, but not the other."

"Are you sure?"

The barkeep nodded. "I try to remember all the men that come in here heeled. I can't always commit them to memory, but it wasn't that long ago when that man came in here."

"You're sure it was him?" Clint asked.

"He walked like his right leg was hurt. He carried a gun and he looked more or less like you described. I even saw him down the street a ways in front of the Ranger Hotel earlier tonight. That place serves a fairly good steak. A bit too much gristle, but that's neither here nor there."

"The Ranger Hotel, you say?"

"I don't know if he's still there or not, but you can see for yourself. He may not even be the man you're after, but it's worth a look."

Clint downed the rest of his beer and nodded. "I was thinking the same thing."

THIRTY-NINE

"Make love to me."

When Acklund had come back into town, he'd been angry at his brother. Actually, he'd been angry at both brothers. Dave was the idiot who'd turned everything into a mess by associating with the likes of Al and Rob, while Mose was the idiot who insisted on trusting those two assholes.

Acklund still wore a scowl on his face as he asked, "What did you say?"

Smiling as if she'd been hoping to repeat herself, Ellie leaned in closer to him and whispered, "Make love to me."

"I don't know about that."

"I've been thinking about this ever since you left."

"But," Acklund cut in, "that was only—"

"I'm tired of thinking," Ellie said as though she didn't even realize he'd been trying to speak to her. "This night has been so good and I don't want it to end. I want it to get better. I want you so much." Suddenly, her eyes snapped open and she asked, "Do you want me, too?"

"Of course I do. I just—"

"Then come to my room," Ellie said happily. She grabbed him by the arm and dragged him to her door. "I don't ever want to forget this night."

Acklund struggled to keep his wits about him. That

became an almost impossible task when Ellie got him into her room, shut the door, and then wrapped her arms around him. Her lips pressed against his and quickly parted. He opened his mouth as well. Once he felt her tongue sliding upon his own and her body grinding against his, there was no going back.

He could feel her smiling against his mouth when he reached around to place his hands upon the small of her back. It didn't take much to get Ellie to push herself even tighter against him. When Acklund moved his hand down, she lifted her leg to rub it against his hip. Letting his instincts take over, Acklund reached under her skirts until he could feel the smooth, warm touch of her skin.

Suddenly, Ellie reached down to tug at his belt. She pulled at the buckle and even let out a little growl when it didn't come loose right away. She quickly had his jeans unfastened so she could pull them down. Ellie tore free of Acklund's hands so she could drop to her knees and wrap her lips around his cock.

It happened so quickly that Acklund nearly lost his footing. Ellie grabbed him roughly with both hands and sucked on him greedily. Her tongue slid up and down along the length of his penis. When he grew harder in her mouth, she sucked on him with even more vigor.

"Slow down, girl," Acklund said. He tried to back away a step, but that only made her want to devour him more. He reached down to pull her head back and hold it there. "I thought you said you didn't want this to end."

It took her a moment, but Ellie soon giggled and dabbed at the corner of her mouth. "Right. I just got carried away."

Acklund helped her to her feet. "Speaking of that . . ." He then picked her up and carried her away to the bed.

She wrapped her arms around him and swung her feet as though she were riding on a porch swing. Acklund set her down and immediately started undressing her. He loosened the ties of her dress and then peeled the clothing from her body. To make things easier, Ellie wriggled out of the dress until she wore nothing but her stockings and a little pair of panties.

"You look pretty as a picture," Acklund said.

Smiling from ear to ear, Ellie stretched out on the bed and posed for him. First she lay on her side so her pert breasts were on display. Then, she rolled onto her stomach and kicked her feet up so her tight little backside wiggled just right.

Acklund couldn't take any more. He crawled onto the bed, pulled her panties off, and buried his face between her legs. Ellie's pussy was wet and waiting for him, so he lapped her up and felt her entire body tremble in response to him. Ellie wrapped her legs around the back of his head so she could hold him close while arching her back.

Suddenly, she sat up and scooted away from him. "Come here," Ellie said as she curled her finger invitingly.

Still able to taste her, Acklund crawled onto the bed.

"Lie down," she commanded.

Acklund may not have known her for very long, but he never would have guessed she could speak so sternly. That tone of voice went well with the look in her eyes. He wasn't about to deny her order, so he lay on his back and watched to see what she would do next.

Ellie remained on all fours and took her time crawling on top of him. Raking her fingernails gently along his leg, she lowered her head like a cat drinking from a saucer of milk. Her tongue flicked out to tease him here and there. Even though she lingered at his rigid pole for a while, it wasn't nearly long enough. Before Acklund could get too upset about her moving on, he felt her mouth work its way along his chest.

Swinging one leg over him, Ellie mounted him and reached down to stroke his penis. She smiled and moaned softly as if touching him was enough to make her feel good. She lifted herself up a bit, guided him between her legs, and settled down again.

The moment Acklund was inside of her, he could feel her body quiver. The lips of her pussy gripped him tightly and only became tighter as they slid along his length. Ellie lifted her head and moaned louder as he drove deeper inside of her. By the time she'd ridden him all the way down, her face was aimed at the ceiling and she was shuddering with a full climax.

All Acklund needed to do was lie back and watch as her face contorted in the grip of her own pleasure before finally settling into a contented smile. When she looked down at him, she looked as though she'd just run a mile to get there.

"Now it's your turn," she said.

Acklund grabbed her hips and pumped up into her. The move caught her by surprise, because Ellie let out a little yelp. She must have liked surprises, because she kept smiling and quickly moved her hips in time to his.

She straightened her back and dragged her fingers through her hair, giving Acklund a perfect view of her tight belly and pert breasts. Her nipples were hard and inviting, so he reached up to play with them. The moment she felt his hands on her, Ellie put her own hands on top of his and begged him not to stop.

Soon, she lowered herself so her face was directly above Acklund's. He wrapped one arm around her and used his other hand to rub the curve of her buttocks. That way, he could pull her close every time he pumped up into her. She moaned in his ear until Acklund swore he could feel the floor rattling beneath the bed. The closer he got to his climax, the more his ears filled with the pounding of blood rushing through his veins.

Then again, that sound may not have been blood in his veins.

The floorboards were definitely rattling and the sounds he heard seemed to be filling the entire room.

Suddenly, the door was forced open and slammed against the wall. Despite everything in him that wanted to get up and get to his gun, Acklund couldn't get himself to move.

FORTY

Clint stormed through the door with his gun already drawn. He quickly realized he wasn't the only one with his gun out of its holster.

"Jesus!" Clint said reflexively when he caught sight of Ellie. Once he took a moment to see who was beneath her, he added, "What in the hell?"

Ellie twisted around to look at him over her shoulder. Despite the fact that Clint had already seen her without a stitch on, she grabbed one of the blankets and pulled it up to cover herself. "Clint? What are you doing?"

"I could ask you the same thing. Do you know who you're . . . who that is?"

Acklund watched Clint intently. One of his arms was outstretched toward the gun belt that lay crumpled on the floor. As Clint stalked toward the bed, the muscles in Acklund's arm strained even more.

"Clint, give us some privacy," Ellie begged.

Using his boot to drag the gun belt toward him, Clint said, "This is one of the men who shot at your house the other night. He's the reason we were holed up and you were so frightened."

"That's enough," Ellie snapped.

Just then, Clint wasn't sure if Ellie was frightened about

what he was saying or if she was worried about what he might
say. Not interested in stirring up anything by letting Acklund
know just how familiar he was with Ellie, Clint picked up the
man's gun belt and draped it over his shoulder. "Get off of
him," he demanded.

"Clint, don't be jealous," she said. "Please, just give us a
moment."

"Ellie! Right now!"

She reflexively jumped at the sharp edge in Clint's voice.
Her bare feet scrambled against the floor, but she was able to
regain her balance and rush over to her clothes. Ellie didn't
drop the blanket until she could immediately pick up her
dress and pull it on.

While she was fussing with her clothes, Clint kept his
Colt aimed at Acklund's head. His glare was strong enough
to keep the man pinned to the mattress. "What did you do to
her?" Clint asked.

"I didn't . . . well . . . I did, but . . ." Acklund stammered.

Ellie rushed over to pull Clint away. She tugged at his
arm, but wasn't strong enough to get him to budge from his
spot. Even so, Ellie kept trying as her hastily buttoned dress
hung precariously from one shoulder. "James is a good
man," she said. "We're in love."

"What?" Clint asked. "Did you hear what I just told you?
This man tried to kill us!"

"You killed my brother!" Acklund said.

Clint turned his attention back to the man. "Are you serious or maybe you're just blind? Your brother snapped his
own damn neck while trying to steal my horse!"

Reluctantly, Acklund nodded. "Yeah. I know. But I was
still worked up when I took them shots at you before. I'm
sorry about that. Dave always was an asshole."

Blinking, Clint found himself at a loss for words. Of all
the things he'd expected to find in this room, this wasn't it.
And of all the things he'd expected Acklund to do, apologize
wasn't one of them.

"At least let James put some clothes on," Ellie requested.

Clint nodded and backed up a step. "Get dressed," he said

to Acklund. "And while you're doing that, you can explain yourself."

"Do you know each other?" Ellie asked.

"Dammit, Ellie, just listen for once, will you?" Clint barked. As soon as he saw the look on her face, Clint regretted speaking to her like that. Before the tears could roll from her eyes, Clint quickly tried to repair the damage he'd caused. "I'm telling you, this man isn't who he says he is. He admitted it himself!"

Acklund sat on the edge of the bed, pulling on his jeans. "He's right, Ellie. I wasn't altogether honest with you before."

Finally, Ellie seemed to hear something that was being said to her. She looked at Acklund and asked, "What do you mean?"

"My name's not James. It's Acklund Winter."

"Go on," Clint urged when he heard Acklund's voice taper off. "Tell her the rest."

Acklund started talking. When he told Ellie about how he'd gotten word that the barber was paying to transport something valuable and that Dave had talked his brothers into stealing it, Clint was just as interested as she was. To Acklund's credit, he gave a fairly accurate account of the first time he'd crossed paths with Clint. Only when he got to the part about Dave's last misstep did Acklund stop for a moment.

After taking a breath, Acklund kept his head down and said, "All three of us were never all good, but Dave was the worst. We were still brothers, though. We backed each other when we could and never thought to take anyone else's side. We didn't go along with Dave every time he went to rob a store or take a run at a stagecoach, but we weren't about to stand in his way.

"Mose tried to protect him just like he protects me. He's the oldest and that's what the oldest brother does. Both of us lost our heads when Dave died like that and we went after Clint to put it right." Shaking his head, Acklund said, "We should've known better and we shouldn't have fired on innocents like that. When we did that, it reminded me of how stupid and reckless Dave always was. Still, I didn't think to put a stop to it until I saw you, Ellie."

She smiled and reached out for his hand. Clint stopped her from getting too close.

"So you've got all the sweet talk now," Clint said, "but that may just be because there's a gun to your head."

"He's always been sweet," Ellie cooed. "From the moment I first saw him."

"Which was when?" Clint asked.

"Not that long ago, but it was long enough," she replied without hesitation.

Clint rolled his eyes. "Oh, for Christ's sake." Even though he didn't want to admit it, Acklund didn't seem particularly dangerous. He hadn't made one move to get Clint's gun or grab Ellie as a hostage. Clint had been prepared to correct Acklund's story when he was recounting past events, but hadn't needed to step in. More than that, Clint could see something in the other man's eyes.

Being able to tell when a man was bluffing at a poker table had saved Clint's life more times than he could count. That skill let him know when a man could be lying or when he intended on making a move against him. It also gave him a good idea when a man wasn't bluffing. Oddly enough, Clint was beginning to trust Acklund Winter.

"So what do we do now?" Clint asked.

Ellie let out a breath and sat down as if she no longer had the strength to stand. "I need to think for a moment." She sighed.

Acklund started to put a hand on her knee, but pulled it back. Looking up at Clint, he said, "You got me dead to rights, but I don't need to tell you that. Whatever you do with me, just let her go."

"I wasn't about to do anything to Ellie," Clint replied.

"Then let her go. She needs to get out of here."

Sensing the urgency in Acklund's voice, Clint asked, "Why? What's the rush?"

"Mose is still out there. He don't want to see reason where Dave was concerned and now he's got some of Dave's friends to back him up. They're coming to kill you tomorrow and they intend on doing a real messy job of it."

FORTY-ONE

Clint knocked on the door to Ellie's house using the side of his foot. After something rustled behind the curtains of the front window, the door was pulled open by Hank. As always, the old man didn't look happy.

"What the hell you doin' here?" Hank slurred. Squinting to get a better look at the man standing beside Clint, he asked, "An' who the hell is this?"

Ellie walked past Clint, Acklund, and her father as if she weren't about to take any guff from any of them. "Have you been drinking?" she asked.

"Yeah. So what? Didn' I see that one before?"

"Yes, you have, Pa," Ellie replied simply. "He's one of the men who shot the house. Can you get some water?"

"What? Huh?" the old man grumbled. He sputtered even more when his daughter put a bucket in his hand and pushed him toward the pump. Despite all the noise he was making, he scooted off to the pump just as he'd been asked to do.

Clint gave Acklund a nudge, which was enough to get him moving into the house. Stepping across the threshold, Acklund let his head hang low and his feet scrape the boards as he walked.

Acklund's gun belt was still slung across Clint's shoulder. During the walk to the house from the Ranger Hotel, Clint had been waiting for Acklund to try to reclaim his weapon or even make a run for an alley along the way. Either one of those moves would have made things a whole lot easier for Clint as far as dealing with the man. Since Acklund had stayed true to his word and behaved himself, Clint was stuck with the problem of what to do with him.

Now that they were inside, Clint could see Hank's shotgun propped against a nearby wall. He tensed his gun arm in preparation to draw once he saw Acklund's eyes drift in that direction. But Acklund didn't even flinch toward the weapon. More than that, he didn't so much as glance at Clint to see if there was an opportunity for him to make a move.

The old man shuffled back into the house and set a bucket of water down near the door. "Did you say this fella shot my house?" he asked.

"How much have you had to drink?" Ellie asked.

"Just enough to make me forget about losin' my little girl."

Still wearing her stern expression, Ellie walked forward to give her father a hug. "I'm still here. See?"

"Still touched in the head is what you are," Hank snapped. "If that man shot my damn house, I ought to shoot his damn head!"

Acklund bristled and lifted his chin. "Hey. Don't talk to her like that."

"Just sit down," Clint said as he clapped a hand on Acklund's shoulder, "and shut up."

Acklund did as he was told.

"This is one of the men that shot your house," Clint said to Hank. "He's also one of the men who tried to shoot me when I was on my way into town. He's also—"

"I love him, Pa," Ellie cut in excitedly. "I honestly do."

"Yeah," Clint said in a level tone that had none of Ellie's excitement. "He's that, too."

Hank looked back and forth between all of them as if his eyes were rattling within their sockets. His face flushed with anger that had become all too familiar to Clint and he tripped over his tongue a few times before he could get any words out. "This . . . this is crazy."

Without making a sound, Clint nodded.

Ellie, on the other hand, couldn't stop smiling. "I know how this sounds, but didn't you always tell me I'd know it when I found the man that was right for me?"

Grudgingly, Hank replied, "Yeah. I suppose I did."

"Well, Clint's a good man but he's not the one. Acklund is. I could feel it when I saw him and I could feel it when we . . ."

Clint cringed, praying that Ellie wasn't dumb enough to get into every last detail.

"When we looked into each other's eyes." Ellie sighed. "I could just feel something special."

Clint had to fight to keep from rolling his eyes, but at least she didn't say anything to get her father riled up again. Hank, on the other hand, didn't try to hold back a thing.

"That's the sappiest bunch of horse manure I've ever heard," the old man grunted. Looking at Acklund, he asked, "I suppose you'll agree with her just to stay on her good side, huh?"

"I agree with her because it's true," Acklund replied. "And I feel the same way."

"Fine," Hank said. "We'll settle this later. Is this why you all came stomping into my house to ruin a perfectly good evening?"

"Partly," Clint replied. "I thought you should know where your daughter was, but there's something else."

"There always is," Hank muttered with a shake of his head.

"It might be a good idea for you to spend the night some-where else," Clint told him. "Actually, you might want to spend tomorrow away from here as well."

"Why?"

"The men who shot up your house may be coming back."

Glaring at Acklund, Hank said, "I thought you said this was one of them men."

"I am," Acklund declared. "But my brother will come back and he's bringing some others to take my place. I don't know for certain he'll come back here, but just to be safe—"

"Safe, hell," Hank interrupted. "Ain't no place really safe. What do you think, Clint? Should I go run and hide?"

Clint needed to take a moment to get over the surprise. Not only had Hank addressed him more or less civilly, but the old man actually seemed interested in a response. Perhaps his last day in Hinterland wouldn't be so difficult after all.

FORTY-TWO

Clint spent the night on the front porch of the Ranger Hotel. It was wedged in between several other shops and businesses and had a good view of Hinterland's Main Street. Clint could see folks coming and going fairly well and the only way to get into the hotel from the back was past a gate that was squeaky enough to wake the dead. Acklund swore up and down that he hadn't mentioned the hotel to his brother, so there wasn't any good reason for Mose or the other two to go there.

It felt peculiar for Clint to put any trust whatsoever into anything Acklund told him. Only a few days ago, the two men were shooting at each other. Now Acklund barely seemed capable of harming a fly. He still wasn't sure how he felt about that.

Stepping outside as if he sensed the storm brewing in Clint's head, Hank pulled up a rocker and sat down next to him. "Thought I was the only one to get up so early," he muttered.

Clint looked up at a sky that was a dull orange color with streaks of bright yellow coming in from the east "It's not that early," he said.

"You should tell that to them two kids."

Smirking, Clint replied, "I don't think they're sleeping."

Hank gritted his teeth and shifted in his rocker. "No need to be so matter-of-fact about it."

"I'm surprised you let them stay within twenty yards of each other."

"Especially after what I put you through?" Hank asked.

"Something like that."

The old man grunted and finally found a comfortable spot in his chair. "The tighter I cinch in the reins on that girl, the more she'll buck. Tell you the truth, I don't feel right about what I did to you. There just weren't a good way out of it."

"You could have just let me go," Clint pointed out.

"Sure, but that'd mean I was wrong."

Hank kept his stern expression on his face for a good couple of seconds. In that time, Clint actually thought the old man was trying to make a point. When Hank finally broke into a chuckle, he slapped Clint on the back and told him, "I wasn't gonna hurt ya. Once Mike got to town, I was gonna turn you loose and watch you run the hell away from here."

"Let me guess. Not a lot of fellows come sniffing around Ellie's door?"

"Too many. That's why I gotta put my foot down." Leaning back to look at the hotel, Hank shook his head. "Seein' you and her like I did . . . I suppose it ruffled my feathers the wrong way."

Clint nodded. "I have a pretty good idea of how you feel." Hank surprised him again by tapping him with the back of his hand. When Clint looked down he saw that the hand was open and waiting to be shaken.

"No hard feelin's?" Hank asked.

Clint shook the old man's hand. "Ellie's a good woman. It's nice to know she's got someone looking out for her. Just try to go easy on Acklund. Something tells me he means the things he says."

"Yeah, I know. I seen too many boys lookin' at my Ellie the wrong way. I recognize when there's somethin' right in their eyes. I jus' don't know about the boy's family."

"Yeah," Clint said. "Hopefully, we'll put that matter to

rest soon enough. Speaking of which, I should find another spot to watch the street before I bring them right to you."

Hank waved at the street as if he were dismissing Mose, Dave's friends, and any other gunmen that might have their sights set on him. "Eh, those boys couldn't find their own asses with a funnel. If they could, they would'a been here by now."

"They can find their guns," Clint pointed out. "That's enough to make them dangerous."

"I put you through enough hell already. The only reason you're still here is because I hog-tied you and shoved a shotgun in your face. If not for that, you would've been gone and probably lost them gunslinging idiots along the way. The least I can do is watch your back now."

"That's downright touching, Hank."

"Then you got a crooked way of thinkin', boy. I'm just trying to set things right. Besides, since I can't keep Ellie away from a man she fancies, I might as well show that man what I can do if he steps out of line. If there is a fight comin', it'll show me what this Acklund is made of."

Clint patted the old man on the shoulder. "You want to put things right, just stay by Ellie and keep her safe. I'll do the rest."

"And if Acklund plays us both for fools?" Hank asked.

"Then I'll make him wish he was never born."

FORTY-THREE

After a quick breakfast, Clint made his way to the Howling Moon Saloon. It was a place that Acklund and Mose had already been to, so he figured there was a chance that Mose and anyone riding with him had visited it again. The barkeep recognized Clint on sight, but hadn't seen the eldest brother.

Clint rode Eclipse down to the mill, over to Hank's house, and then past Aunt Iris's cottage. None of those places were infested with gunmen, so he headed back to the Ranger Hotel. Acklund was waiting for him outside.

"Told you they wouldn't be here," Acklund said. "They mean to catch you when there's more folks about."

"Then why don't you take me to where they are," Clint demanded. "That way we won't have to worry about Ellie or Hank getting hurt."

"Fine with me. Just let me get to my horse."

The Ranger Hotel had a small stable behind it at the other end of a narrow alley that led from the street. Clint watched Acklund disappear down the alley and waited to hear the loud squeak of the gate. He tightened his grip on Eclipse's reins, preparing himself to chase Acklund down if he decided to make a run for it.

Clint heard the squeak of the gate.

After that, he heard a horse fidgeting before trotting through the gate again.

Narrowing his eyes, Clint eased his hand toward his holster. The stitches in his gun arm were healing up and he'd already become accustomed to the nagging pain. He'd worked the kinks out well enough to draw without a hitch, but he kept his hand close to the Colt's grip just to be on the safe side.

There were heavy steps coming down the alley, announcing Acklund's presence as he rode back to where Clint was waiting. As soon as he got a look at Clint's face, Acklund narrowed his eyes into a mean glare.

"What's the matter, Clint? Ellie's pa tell you to bury me under this hotel?"

Keeping his hand within a few inches of the Colt, Clint replied, "Just making sure you intend on doing what we agreed on."

"I said I'd take you to Mose's camp and that's what I'm gonna do."

Clint had asked the favor over breakfast in the few seconds when Ellie wasn't gazing lovingly at Acklund's face. The man hadn't needed much time before accepting the proposal. After that, Ellie took Acklund for herself and didn't let him go. At the time, Clint thought that Acklund seemed earnest enough in his reply. But ever since then, Clint couldn't stop wondering if he was making a mistake.

Everything Clint heard from Acklund made it seem that he was being honest with him.

Everything Acklund did fell into line with that. If Acklund had wanted to take a shot at Clint, there had been plenty of opportunities. Clint had even made sure that Acklund kept his gun so he could make his move if that's what he'd wanted to do. But Acklund had either truly lost his need to avenge his brother or he was too smart to go up against Clint when he was looking for it.

As if reading the thoughts rushing through Clint's head, Acklund locked eyes with him and asked, "You want to even things up for what happened before? You want to hurt me since I hurt you?"

"My arm's doing just fine," Clint replied.

"Then why are you looking at me like you mean to put a bullet in my back?"

"If I'd wanted you dead, you already would be. I'm just not sure you've only got Ellie's interests at heart."

"This ain't just about her."

"That's right," Clint said. "It's about your brother. He's still dead and I'm still alive. You want me to believe you just came to peace with that?"

When Clint said those words, he kept his voice steady as a rock and cold as ice. He knew they'd cut straight through Acklund, because that was exactly what Clint intended. If Acklund was going to make a move, he would make it then.

Clint felt a bit of pain from the stitches in his elbow as he got ready to draw and fire, but Acklund didn't even twitch toward his own gun.

"What happened to Dave was his own damn fault," Acklund said. "I'm only leading you to Mose's camp because I don't want any of those crazy friends of my brother's to hurt Ellie or Hank. I also don't want anything to happen to Mose."

"He's out to kill me," Clint pointed out.

"And he'll simmer down once those other two outlaws are gone."

"What if he doesn't?"

Acklund drew a breath and steeled himself. "Then whatever happens will be his fault. You promise me that you'll give Mose a chance to change his mind. If you put a bullet in him at your first chance, I'll see to it I put one into you. I've already lost one brother. I won't lose another."

It was a rare occasion that Clint respected a man who threatened his life, but he couldn't help doing just that. Nodding, Clint took his hand away from his holster. "Let's go."

FORTY-FOUR

Eclipse had barely hit his stride when Acklund signaled for
them to slow down. He pulled back on his reins and Clint did
the same, while watching for any sign of an attack. All Clint
could see was Acklund pointing toward a stand of trees not
too far away. When he waited for a second, Clint could hear
what he thought was rowdy laughing up ahead.

Normally, Clint would have liked to send his partner
ahead to try to circle the camp before Clint rode straight into
it. That would increase their chances thanks to a simple yet
classic strategy. But Acklund wasn't Clint's typical sort of
partner. In fact, Clint was just as concerned about him as he
was about whoever was at that camp.

Both men rode forward, watching each other as much as
they did the trees in front of them. Before he got close
enough to see the camp, Clint saw a figure step away from
the trees and then dart behind them again.

Clint snapped his reins and prepared himself for a fight.

"That you, brother?" Mose said as he stepped out from
the thick stand of trees.

Acklund pulled back on his reins a bit and shouted, "It's
me, all right! Send those outlaws home and let's be done
with this. We've taken this too far already."

Mose hardly seemed to hear his brother. Instead, his eyes

were fixed upon Clint and he shifted his feet to take a lower sideways stance.

Sensing the big man's intentions, Clint pulled back on his reins and positioned his hand so he could draw at a moment's notice.

"What are you talkin' about?" Mose asked.

Acklund straightened up and practically stood in his stirrups as he roared, "You know what I'm talking about! It's what I've been saying since this whole damn thing got so far out of hand. It's over, damn it!"

Raising his arm to level a finger at Clint, Mose said, "This ain't over till he's dead."

Before Clint could say a word to that, the trees on either side of Mose exploded in a flurry of fallen leaves and thundering hooves. Two horses busted out from where they'd been hiding on the left and right side of the trees. The men riding the two horses yelled like a pack of wild Indians and immediately started firing at Clint.

Even though the shots were fast and out of control, they were all hissing in Clint's direction. Standing in the middle of a hailstorm like that was just asking to be hit. Having already been felled by his share of lucky shots, Clint snapped his reins and steered Eclipse to the left. He didn't have to think about drawing his gun. Clint's reflexes acted for him and, amid a biting pain from the stitches in his elbow, the modified Colt was in his grasp.

Leaning forward over Eclipse's neck, Clint only had to keep hold of the reins so he could snap or pull back on them. He steered by nudging in either direction with his knees and the Darley Arabian responded as if he could read Clint's thoughts.

For the moment, Clint let Eclipse run as fast as he pleased. More wild shots hissed through the air above his head and on either side, while Clint took his time to get a clearer line of fire. The man on the horse closest to him had bushy hair that waved in the breeze like the treetops behind him. His mouth was open and curled into a wide smile as he emptied one pistol and then drew another to replace it.

Firing one shot toward Rob, Clint gauged his next angle based on the speed of both horses along with the reaction of his wounded arm. Despite a throbbing pain that went all the way up to his shoulder, Clint's wound wasn't giving him any trouble. Rob's horse whinnied at the gunfire, but didn't seem spooked by it. That didn't hold true for the man in the horse's saddle.

Rob shouted something at Clint, but his words were swallowed up in all the noise. Clint's first shot was high, but the next one clipped Rob across the back of his neck. The yelp he let out after that was plenty loud enough to be heard through all the other sounds.

Clint tapped his heels against Eclipse's sides to get the stallion to move even faster. The Darley Arabian bolted forward without missing a beat, allowing Clint to ride around the backside of the trees just in time to catch the second rider attempting to flank him.

Al wasn't in as much of a hurry as his partner. Sitting tall in the saddle, Al brought a rifle to his shoulder and fired off a shot. As the round whipped past Clint's head, Al levered in another and did his best to steady his aim.

Rather than waste a shot trying to rattle the man, Clint held onto his reins and put Eclipse through a series of sharp turns before passing Al's horse altogether. Once he had a little space between them, Clint pulled hard on Eclipse's reins to turn the stallion completely around.

Any other rider would have been thrown by the maneuver. On any other horse, turning so sharply at such a fast speed was foolish at best and deadly at the worst. But Clint and Eclipse had been together long enough for one to respond to the other as if they were a single living thing.

Eclipse sent a wave of dirt flying as he skidded and turned at the same time.

Clint felt his momentum carrying him off his saddle, but he held on as best he could. His legs clamped over Eclipse's sides and his wounded right arm cried for mercy, but Clint was able to stay off the ground. In fact, he found himself even higher in the air as Eclipse reared up on his hind legs and churned his forelegs in the air to complete his turn.

Now that he was facing the other rider, Clint could see Al no more than thirty yards away. Al hadn't tried to turn his whole horse around, but was obviously surprised that Clint had pulled off that feat. Al twisted his upper body around to take aim with his rifle, but fired off a shot that sliced through the air well ahead of Eclipse's nose. If Clint had kept moving in his previous direction, Al would have led his target perfectly. As it was, Al had to take a second to lever another round into his chamber and readjust his aim.

That short amount of time was all Clint needed. Before Eclipse could drop back down onto all fours, Clint extended his arm and squeezed his trigger. Al jerked in his saddle as soon as the modified Colt bucked against Clint's palm. Just to be certain, Clint fired again. That shot knocked Al to the ground and allowed his horse to take off on its own.

Letting out a breath that sounded like steam being released from a piston, Eclipse regained his balance and dropped back down to all fours. As soon as his front hooves hit the earth, he was off and running once more.

Retracing his steps, Clint rode back around the trees until he could see Acklund and Mose tearing into each other with their bare hands. He wasn't as concerned about the two brothers, however, as he was about the other gunman that had ridden away and disappeared. Clint steered clear of the brothers as he continued to circle around the trees. Since he still couldn't find a trace of Rob, Clint knew there was only one place for the man to be. He could also smell the trap the gunman was hoping to spring as though Rob had sent up smoke signals.

Obviously, Clint was supposed to charge into the trees and leave himself open to an ambush that Rob could spring from any number of hiding places. More than willing to oblige, Clint pointed Eclipse's nose toward the trees and snapped his reins.

Just before Eclipse passed into the cluster of timber, Clint swung one leg over and launched himself toward some bushes and tall grass sprouting at the base of one tree. He hit the bushes on his side, getting plenty of scratches and bruises for his trouble. Clint still recovered quickly enough to hear the shots fired from deeper within the clearing and to trace them back to their source.

Rob was firing wildly, but he was also shooting high enough to hit anyone on a horse's back. By the time Eclipse was close enough for him to see the empty saddle on his back, Rob had already reached the end of his rope. He snapped his eyes toward the spot where Eclipse had broken through the trees, only to find Clint standing there looking right back at him.

The Colt barked twice, sending the contents of Rob's skull through the air in a red mist.

Clint whistled for Eclipse and heard the Darley Arabian slow down so he could circle back around. Instead of waiting for the horse to get to him, Clint reloaded his pistol and walked to the spot where Acklund and Mose were fighting. By the looks of it, they'd both landed some healthy blows.

One punch from Acklund sent Mose staggering back half a step. Unfortunately for the younger of the two, this gave Mose some room to cock his right arm back and launch a powerful swing at Acklund's jaw. Mose's fist slammed into Acklund's face, dropping him like a sack of oats. When he hit the ground, Acklund stayed there.

Turning toward the sound of Clint's steps, Mose growled, "All right, asshole. Let's settle this."

FORTY-FIVE

Clint had his gun in hand, but that didn't seem to bother Mose in the least. Walking forward, Clint nodded. "You want to settle this? Sounds good to me." With that, Clint tossed his gun away and balled up his fists.

For a man Mose's size, he moved awfully quick. He leaned toward Clint and snapped his left hand out to connect with Clint's ribs. There was another punch hot on the heels of that one, but Clint was fast enough to step back and swat it away.

Flicking his right hand out like a whip, Clint took a swing at Mose's face. Clint's knuckles barely scraped against their target, but the punch was only meant to set the bigger man up for the second. As soon as Mose ducked away from his right hand, Clint sent his left out in a low, powerful uppercut that pounded against Mose's stomach. Clint felt as if he'd punched a wall.

Mose answered the punch with one of his own that was aimed at the same spot on Clint's body. Unlike Clint's punch, however, this one caused Clint to double over and let out a pained grunt. Before Clint had a chance to straighten up and suck in another breath, Mose dropped his other hand straight down like a hammer to smash into Clint's shoulder.

Gritting his teeth as his bones rattled under his skin, Clint threaded his fingers together and swung both hands like he was swinging an ax. The powerful blow caught Mose in the middle of his torso, just beneath his rib cage. Even though the impact sent the big man back a step or two, Mose was quick to come straight at Clint once again.

First, Mose took a swing at Clint as if he meant to knock his head off. When Clint ducked under the punch, Mose slapped his hand onto Clint's shoulder to hold him down as he brought his knee up.

Clint didn't see the knee coming and he barely felt it land. All of a sudden, a loud thump filled his ears and his feet were out from under him. Clint's body went numb and he didn't even know he'd been off the ground until he dropped back onto it.

Straining to clear his vision, Clint pulled in a few breaths and tried to get his bearings. He realized he'd landed within a few feet of his pistol, so Clint tried to get to the Colt before Mose squashed him like a bug.

"Go on and shoot me, murderer!" Mose shouted.

Clint pounded his fist against the ground and pulled himself up. When he got to his feet, he left the Colt where it had landed. "I didn't murder your brother! He fell off . . . if you don't know that by now, I'm not going to waste any more breath on the subject."

Mose stood like one of the trees behind him. His chest swelled like a set of bellows as he sucked in some wind and he propped both bloody fists on his hips. "Yeah," he wheezed. "I know he fell."

"You do?" Clint asked. "Then why go through all of this?"

It took a few seconds for Mose to catch his breath, but finally he replied, "I kind of got caught up. It weren't until I had a chance to clear my head that I could see things clearer."

"And when did that happen?"

Licking the corner of his mouth that either Clint or Acklund had bloodied, Mose grinned and said, "About a minute or two ago."

Clint narrowed his eyes and watched the big man carefully. "So what about settling this?"

"Far as I'm concerned, it's settled. Hell, this is how me and my brothers settle just about everything."

At that time, Acklund stirred and let out a pained groan. He got to his feet, saw Clint, and immediately said, "Don't neither one of you move!"

Mose walked over to his brother and helped him steady himself. "Don't fret, little brother. Me and Clint settled things."

Acklund looked over at Clint. Apparently, the sight of Clint's battered face told him all he needed to know. "You finally going to let this rest?"

Mose nodded. "Dave wasn't even shot, so I guess it could've been an accident. Ma always said he'd get himself killed anyhow."

"Jesus." Acklund sighed. "You're a real piece of work."

Clint picked up his gun and dropped it into his holster. Eclipse was trotting over to him, but he walked over to the two brothers before the stallion arrived. Once he had both men's attention, Clint said, "I'm sorry about your brother."

There was plenty more he could say, especially when it came to laying blame about who attacked whom or how many shots had been fired, but Clint knew that wouldn't do anyone any good. The two brothers knew it as well and they simply nodded.

"You still want to set this right?" Clint asked.

"I want to put this to rest," Acklund replied.

"Good. Then come along with me."

FORTY-SIX

When Clint rode up to the Ranger Hotel, Hank stormed out like he was about to raise some hell. "What the hell was the meaning of that?" the old man snarled as he looked at Clint as though Acklund and Mose weren't right beside him. "We were supposed to work together! You weren't supposed to go off on yer own like a damned fool!"

"Sorry," Clint said. "Things got settled without you."

Finally, Hank looked at the two men riding with Clint. Scowling at Mose, he asked, "Is that the other one that shot up my place?"

"Yes," Clint replied. "I brought him back to answer for what he did. If you want to hand him over to the law, that's your call."

Mose shifted in his saddle and glanced over to find Deputy Cale looking at him as he walked out of the hotel's restaurant.

Before Hank could say another word, Ellie rushed outside. "Acklund! You're back!"

"I ought to hand both of you over to the law," Hank groused.

Pulling in a surprised breath, Ellie ran to stand between Acklund and her father as if she were shielding the younger man from a bullet. "No! I love him!"

Mose chuckled, while Clint rolled his eyes.

"What're your intentions toward my girl?" Hank asked.

Acklund met the old man's glare and said, "I love her, too, sir."

"So is this settled?" Clint asked.

Mose rubbed his nose and grunted, "I just want a drink."

"Then buy me one, too," Hank snapped. "And fix the window you shot. After that, we're settled."

Clint looked between the men and saw all of them nodding to seal the deal. "Good. It's settled."

Digging in his pockets, Hank grumbled, "Speaking of that, I owe you for the rest of that flower picture."

"Keep it," Clint replied. "Consider it my wedding gift. It'll be delivered to you shortly."

"Wedding?" Acklund gasped as the color drained from his face.

"Can you stay for a while longer, Clint?" Ellie asked. "Please?"

"I don't think so," Clint told her. "Just do me a favor. On your wedding night, remember to lock your door."

Watch for

RED WATER

325th novel in the exciting GUNSMITH series
from Jove

Coming in January!

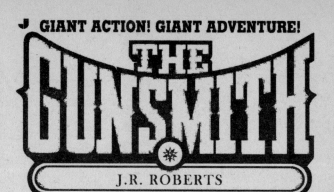

GIANT ACTION! GIANT ADVENTURE!

THE GUNSMITH

J.R. ROBERTS

penguin.com